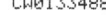

A FLORA FARRINGTON ROMANTIC MYSTERY

# FLORA'S COTSWOLD CHRISTMAS MYSTERY

Published in the UK in 2025 by The Cotswold Writer Press

Copyright © Anna A Armstrong 2025

Anna A Armstrong has asserted their right under
the Copyright, Designs and Patents Act, 1988,
to be identified as the author of this work.

All rights reserved. No part of this book may be reproduced, stored in a retrieved system or transmitted, in any form or by any means, electronic, mechanical, scanning, photocopying, recording or otherwise, without the prior permission of the author and publisher.

Paperback ISBN: 978-1-7394217-8-6
eBook ISBN: 978-1-7394217-9-3

Cover design by Viktoriya Avramova/SpiffingCovers
Typeset by Spiffing Covers

A FLORA FARRINGTON ROMANTIC MYSTERY

# FLORA'S COTSWOLD CHRISTMAS MYSTERY

ANNA A. ARMSTRONG

*For my three lovely daughters and their wonderful husbands.*

# CAST OF CHARACTERS

The Honourable Flora Farrington – wealthy war widow and mother of Tony (b.1910 with blue eyes and black hair like his father) and Debo (b.1914 with brown curly hair and brown eyes like her mother). Flora is in her thirties, petite and darker than is the fashion.
Dorothy the dachshund – impeccable in both her looks and breeding.
Inspector Busby – early thirties. Flora suspects he is a few years younger than her.
Nanny – younger than she looks. Irish, hard whisky drinking, cigar smoking, carpetbag in hand. Knitter and no-nonsense. She has been with Flora since she was a baby.

**Flora's Household – Farrington Hall in the Cotswolds**
Mrs Wilkes - Housekeeper/cook.
Mavis and Gladys – Flora's excitable maids.
Mr Bert, old as the hills – Gardener.
Butler – Roberts, small, lithe and agile. A classic suave 'silver fox'. Both Flora and Roberts himself think of him as more an 'honorary' butler than a normal 'mere' servant. They met in the Spring when Flora was in France.

**Derek Adams' household:**
Maud (deceased) – an old schoolfriend of Flora's – they have had little contact over the years and in reality, never really cared for each other.
Derek Adams – Maud's husband – slicked-back hair and with poor taste in tweed. He is probably around fifty.

Nurse Susan Smythson is an efficient nurse in her late twenties. A handsome lady with violet eyes and chestnut hair.
Mrs Scrubs – Housekeeper - indeterminate age, possibility in her forties. Secretive and desiccated.
Paul Draycott – extremely talented gardener but ruined by the war.
Claire Draycott – Paul's wife – aged twenty-four.
Betty Draycott – Paul and Claire's cute toddler.

**Others:**
Dr Victor Honour – austere and reserved. He had been a medical officer during the war and bears the scars down the left side of his face.
Amanda Honour – Dr Honour's mother – she has cold grey eyes and an icy personality.
Lady Robin Clarke – goodlooking, wealthy and ruthless.
Mrs Joan Pie – a warm and motherly lady who runs the children's home.
Lavinia – Flora's goddaughter – young, beautiful, orphaned and wealthy.
Great Aunt Gigi – flamboyant and fabulous.
Pierre and Anton Beau Frere - Great Aunt Gigi's Beautiful Boys.
Jaqueline Bernard – annoyingly youthful and attractive (to Flora's mind) who knew Busby as a child. She is presently working as a French governess for Colonel Ford and Mrs Ford's three daughters.

# CHAPTER 1

## 9<sup>TH</sup> DECEMBER 1924
## THE POSSIBILITY OF MURDER

'Flora, please tell me that it wasn't you who murdered Maud.'

In her surprise, Flora swerved her Morgan sports car and exclaimed, '*Nanny*! Why on earth would you think I'd do such a thing?'

Bringing the car back under control, she glanced over to where Nanny's ample form was squashed into the small car seat. Dressed with her long black cloak over her outdated dress and with a hat pinned to her wild grey curls, she looked as if she belonged to the Victorian age rather than the modernity of the 1920s. With both Dorothy the dachshund and her ever-present red carpetbag perched on her knee, she looked less than comfortable.

Calmly, Nanny replied, 'How else are you going to get to spend time with that lovely Inspector Busby?' While Flora spluttered with indignation, Nanny's small black eyes twinkled, and in a matter-of-fact tone she added, 'I'm not saying that I'd blame you. After all, you have been a widow for a long time and Busby is gorgeous.'

Dorothy yapped, *Amen to that*!

Flora skilfully overtook a heavy horse pulling a cart and declared, 'But still, Nanny, surely you don't think I'm capable of putting weights in the pockets of her dressing gown and leaving her to drown in a freezing ornamental lake?'

Nanny considered the point for what Flora considered to be an unnecessarily long time. 'Well, you were never very keen on her when you were at school together.'

'Really, Nanny!' They drove on for a bit in silence before Flora continued, 'She really couldn't have chosen a more inconvenient time to die, what with Christmas just around the corner. The children will be home for the holidays in the next day or two, then not long after that we have the fireworks party, and then the Lords and Ladies ball, not to mention Great Aunt Gigi's coming to stay.'

Nanny chose to ignore the prospect of Great Aunt Gigi's visit. Instead, she smiled and remarked, 'I always rather enjoy the Lords and Ladies ball. It's grand having the lords and ladies waiting on the staff.'

'Except there aren't any lords and ladies in the village. I am the nearest thing and I am only an Hon,' said Flora as she swept a stray brown curl out of her eyes with one gloved hand while keeping the other hand firmly on the steering wheel. She couldn't imagine how it had managed to escape her tight-fitting red hat.

Nanny sniffed. 'Anyways, I doubt Maud was planning on getting murdered just now.'

'Probably not,' conceded Flora.

'And we're discounting the notion she might have taken her own life.'

Flora frowned. 'Shouldn't think so – she was never low-spirited and she lacked the imagination. Besides, with a potful of money – and, as she told me in her last letter, a new husband who was the last thing in doting – why would she? Isn't it ridiculous that since she moved into the village a few weeks ago, the only contact I have had with her is through letters? I haven't even met her new husband.' She was silent for a moment as she slowed for a sharp corner. 'Although, in my defence, Maud was only here for a heartbeat before she had to have her appendix out and didn't want visitors.'

'Word in the village is that Derek Adams is an affable sort of a chap, whereas Maud was unfriendly.'

Flora sighed. 'She always was a bit of a pill. All elbows, if you know what I mean. I think at the heart of the problem was that she always had more money than brains.'

'A bit like your goddaughter.'

'Which one?'

'Lavinia.'

'Gosh, you are right! They both have – or in Maud's case, had – the same wide-eyed prettiness and giddy personality. While we are talking about Lavinia, did I mention that she's popping in for tea today?'

Nanny nodded. 'And then will she be staying for the fireworks, ball and Christmas?'

'Sort of. I believe she'll be popping up and down to London for the odd festive party.'

Nanny wriggled on her seat. 'Thank goodness we are nearly there. Your driving is more suitable for the racetrack at Brooklands than for taking your old nanny on an outing. I've been meaning to ask: tell me, where did Maud's money come from?'

'Her father made a fortune in textiles up north and then he made even more during the war. He had the government contract for socks, or was it Macinoshes? I have an idea there was a bit of a scandal with that – something about substandard quality. Anyway, he conveniently died of a heart attack leaving his partner to face the music. He killed himself.'

'What? I thought you said he had a heart attack?'

Flora sighed. 'It was Maud's father who had a heart attack and Maud's father's business partner who had to face the music.'

Nanny nodded. 'And it was this business partner who took his life as the result of the scandal?'

'That's right!' said Flora as she slowed down to overtake a group of children walking along the side of the road.

'But despite the scandal, Maud still inherited a fortune?' queried Nanny

'Exactly. More money than she knows what to do with. And here we are,' said Flora as they turned into a driveway.

Nanny frowned. 'Well there doesn't seem to be much of a mystery around her demise then. If it was murder, the husband must have done it.'

'Nanny, you are always on the ball, solving murders before teatime, but we still have to prove it.'

Nanny laughed and returned to an earlier topic. 'Which will mean you can spend more time with Busby.'

Flora flushed – even the tops of her ears went pink. Her mouth went inexplicably dry and she had to swallow before she could speak. 'Don't be ridiculous!' she stammered without much conviction as she brought the car to a stop.

Nanny gave a low chuckle; obviously she wasn't convinced.

Flora stepped out of the car and stood up straight. Diminutive, at just a smidge over five foot, she was slim and fit. She may have a darker complexion than was fashionable but people only tended to notice the warmth of her smile. It was as she smoothed down her dress after the drive that she had a sudden qualm of doubt. 'Oh Nanny you don't think this dress, coat and hat ensemble is a bit inappropriate for a house in mourning, do you?'

Nonchalantly, Nanny regarded her. 'Totally inappropriate, child. Since when has bright red been suitable for visiting the bereaved? Still, it's too late now.'

Flora glanced down at Dorothy, who was looking very dashing in her matching red collar and lead. The dachshund looked back at her with sparkling black eyes and wagged her tail enthusiastically. 'And I probably shouldn't have brought you, either, however much you fussed not to be left at home.' She straightened herself and took a deep breath. 'Still, as Nanny says, it's too late now.'

Nanny surveyed the modern, square house. Its name was carved and painted on a sign: 'Heavenly Haven'.

Nanny sniffed. 'Frightfully of the moment. Can't say I care much for it but I suppose it would be easy to run.'

Flora agreed. 'It *is* modern.' In her eyes, when it came to architecture, there could be no greater criticism than to be deemed modern. She tilted her head on one side, regarding the house critically. 'It looks so stark and harsh. Why on earth didn't they use the soft-coloured local stone?'

It was square and sparse. The house itself was off-white with incongruous green shutters dressing the windows. The front door was elevated by a generous porch.

Thoughtfully Flora said, 'The house is not exactly small, but it is surprisingly modest considering Maud's wealth.'

Nanny nodded while Flora turned her attention to the immaculate garden and thought of her own garden's sad state. She sighed. 'I must say the grounds are sensational. My own gardener, Mr Bert, is a poppet but I'm afraid he's long past creating a masterpiece like this.'

As they approached the house they noticed the front door had been left ajar, despite the winter weather. Through, the open front door they heard raised voices. They glanced at each other with raised eyebrows and gave each other a significant look.

Flora smiled and said solemnly, 'Oh dear, Nanny, we appear to have come at an inopportune moment.'

Nanny nodded and gave her a grin. 'And if we edge a step or two to the left, we should be able to see and hear everything.'

As ever, Nanny was quite right. Through the open front door they had an excellent view of the combatants. Flora was pleased that, for once, Dorothy kept a discreet silence.

Flora whispered, 'I know Dr Victor Honour of course.' She nodded toward the man. He was around six foot in height, with scarring on the left side of his face – yet another relic of the war. Like most of the village, Flora held him in high regard. His austere manner meant he was admired rather than held in affection. He did general practice but was known to have a dream of setting up a nursing home to soothe the souls of the men who had come back from the war scarred in the mind.

Flora indicated the young woman in front of him. 'But who is that?'

She wore a starched grey nurse's uniform and was nearly as tall as the doctor. She had dark chestnut hair and was what was termed handsome rather than pretty. The fine lines around her eyes suggested to Flora an age around the late thirties.

Nanny just had time to hiss, 'That's some fancy nurse, I believe her name is Nurse Smythson. She happened to be down from London when Maud had her emergency appendix op.'

The doctor was breathing heavily, his fists were clenched and when he spoke his voice shook. 'Nurse Smythson, the medication

I left in your care has definitely not been handled correctly. The sedation has been over-used.'

Nurse Smythson raised her chin. There was a faint flush above her strong cheekbones. 'Dr Honour, as I have already told you, I only used the vials of morphine as you directed.' Her voice was strained, showing only the slightest tremor of emotion.

His jaw tensed. 'Then explain the missing ones.'

Under his intimidating stare, Nurse Smythson hung her head, and the tone of her voice dropped. 'I can't.'

It was at that moment that an older man slunk in. Flora guessed this must be Maud's husband, Derek Adams. His suit was brash but crumpled, his hair was dyed and pomaded. Narrow-shouldered and smooth-jawed, there were shadows beneath his eyes and his face was unnaturally pallid. When he spoke, his voice was barely above a feeble whisper. 'Dr Honour, I must protest. I strongly object to you implying any misconduct on Susan's – I mean Nurse Smythson's – behalf. Her conduct in the time she has been here has been exemplary. My dear wife's death is nothing but a tragic accident.'

His voice had caught on the word 'death'. For a moment he was overcome with emotion but quickly collected himself. 'I have been constantly impressed by her patience. My darling Maud could be a little trying at times and Nurse Smythson only ever showed her compassion and understanding.'

Nurse Susan Smythson threw him a grateful look which lifted her face and made Flora revise the age she had guessed. Perhaps she was in her late twenties.

Flora and Nanny were fascinated but their sleuthing was interrupted by a sharp query in an accusatory tone. 'Can I help you?'

They found themselves confronted by an exceptionally tall and thin old woman, with grey hair in a tight bun under an austere and ugly hat. *Goodness!* thought Flora. *She looks just like that pet tortoise I had as a child! She has the same bulging, rheumy eyes, no chin – and talk about a crepey neck! This must be the housekeeper; I believe her name is Mrs Scrubs.*

Flora blushed. Nanny was made of sterner stuff, and brazenly, looked her up and down.

Dr Honour and Nurse Smythson stopped arguing, startled into silence as the three came to the front door. They stared at Nanny and Flora. Even Derek Adams blinked at them.

'What-ho!' stammered Flora with a weak smile.

At that moment, a saviour appeared in the unlikely form of Mrs Honour, the doctor's mother. She was a familiar and forceful figure in both Flora's and the village's life.

*I never thought the day would come when I would actually be pleased to see her!*

She was nearly as tall as the scowling housekeeper, but far more elegant in both dress and demeanour. Flora had known the imposing older woman for many years but she had always remained an acquaintance rather than a friend. Mrs Honour wore her snow-white hair swept up in an elegant chignon, with the suggestion of a chic hat pinned to one side. She was wearing a dove-grey dress that was à la mode, with its dropped waist and higher hem.

Flora glanced at Mrs Honour's costume with a silent sigh. *Trust Mrs Honour to choose a colour so much more suitable for a house in mourning than my dashing red.*

Mrs Honour's return gaze clearly stated that she was thinking, *What in the world are you doing, visiting a house in mourning in* that *costume?*

But all she actually said was, 'Mrs Farrington, I see you are here, like me, to pay your respects.'

Exultant at this opt-out-of-an-embarrassing-moment suggestion, Flora mumbled, 'Rather!'

Dr Honour's lips were set in a firm line. 'Mother, now is not the time.'

Mrs Honour cast a dismissive glance at her son. 'Victor, you must allow me to be the best judge of what is and is not a good time.' Seamlessly, she turned to the housekeeper and with a quiet, commanding voice demanded, 'Mrs Scrubs, be so good as to make us some tea. We will have it in the drawing room.' She bestowed a charming smile on the grieving widower. 'Mr Adams, If you will kindly show us the way.'

She strode forwards with Flora following meekly in her wake. *Gosh! It must be heavenly to be so audacious.*

As they headed towards the drawing room, Nanny quietly followed the housekeeper to the kitchen.

The drawing room was rectangular and bland. The fireplace was mean and small; Flora could tell at a glance that it was not big enough to ever provide a roaring blaze. The rest of the room was equally uninspiring. It boasted magnolia walls and the curtains were insipid. The chairs were of recent design and comfortable, which was more than could be said for the company.

Flora noted the small array of Christmas cards on display. *Very festive, but I'd rather not have the reminder that I haven't started mine yet.* She brightened. *It's probably too late now, so I needn't bother.* She turned her attention back to her host.

Derek Adams was polite. Even in his dishevelled state of mourning, with his hint of stubble and his shirt not fully tucked in he managed to say all the right things. 'How kind of both of you ladies to come. Mrs Honour, I know how busy you are, so thoughtful of you to make the time to visit. Mrs Farrington? Ah yes! If only we were meeting under happier circumstances. My dear Maud always spoke so fondly of your schooldays together.'

To Flora's delight, Mrs Honour soon proved to be a positive bulldog of determination when it came to questioning Derek over Maud's demise. Primly poised, sitting very erect on the edge of her seat, the older lady regarded their host with cool grey eyes. 'Now, Derek, what in the world was Maud thinking of? I mean, wandering down to the lake in nothing more than her nightie and dressing gown at that hour of the morning?'

The implied criticism of his late wife seemed to affect Derek deeply; his lined face contorted in distress. *Oh goodness, the poor man looks stricken. I am a worm for gleefully prying into Maud's demise. Sometimes my curiosity is a curse.*

With a sigh, he admitted, 'And barefoot.'

'Barefoot?' exclaimed Flora, all remorse forgotten. 'But

Maud always had a bit of a phobia about going around barefoot. She kicked up a stink when Gracie Pearl and Gertie Arbuckle hid her slippers in Matron's aspidistra.' She felt a zing of excitement. *This is confirmation that Maud was murdered – she would never have ventured outside without her feet suitably clad. Of course, it could be argued that galoshes would be even more suitable wear than slippers.*

Mrs Honour was uninterested in Gracie and Gertie's adventures with Matron's aspidistra and spoke over Flora. 'I understand she had her appendix out two weeks ago – could that have affected the balance of her mind?'

Derek ran a heavy hand through his grey hair and slowly shook his head. 'I really couldn't say. Dr Honour and Nurse Smythson performed the operation on the kitchen table. We were so fortunate Nurse Smythson was on hand – she's had a lot of theatre experience at that big London hospital, I forget its name.'

Mrs Honour sniffed and said tartly, 'I hardly think the presence of some nurse was of any significance. My son is truly brilliant. His talent is sadly wasted in this backwater. I keep urging him to open rooms in Harley Street but…' She grimaced before returning her hawk-like gaze on Derek. 'I understand you were away from home when the incident occurred?'

Derek appeared to be only half listening; he was staring at his shoes. He nodded absently. 'I had pressing business in Shrewsbury and only arrived back as—' his voice caught, '—as Maud's body was being carried up from the pond.' He took a couple of steadying breaths. 'I should never have left her, but the business matter was urgent and I thought that with Susan, Nurse Smythson, here… I never imagined—'

'Quite,' declared Mrs Honour. Her grey eyes were cold as ice, her thin lips a rigid line. 'I must say she couldn't have chosen a more inconvenient time, what with Christmas in two weeks. We have the fireworks party and the Lords and Ladies ball before that.'

Derek murmured a weak apology while Flora mused, *Gosh Nanny was right; it does sound rather callous when one points out the trickiness of Maud's timing. I must try to be a better person.*

Mrs Honour was now in full flow. 'I suppose we will have to cancel the village's traditional Christmas fireworks.' She tutted and shook her head in a disapproving way. 'Such a shame as everyone was so looking forward to it, especially the children. Still, it can't be helped. We can hardly hold the fireworks party by your ornamental lake under the circumstances.' She did some more tutting and head shaking; this time it was laced with regret. 'Pity – fireworks always look magnificent when reflected over a body of water. But like I said, it can't be helped. If only we could find a new venue but at this late date and so close to Christmas, I fear that is impossible.'

Derek's shoulders drooped more and more with each phrase of her accusatory speech and his hollow eyes sank further into his face. Weakly he murmured, 'I really am most terribly sorry.'

Flora felt her heart constrict as she regarded the poor man. Impulsively she declared, 'No problem at all. Please don't give it a second thought. We can have the fireworks party at Farrington Hall. It's a little further from the village but we can lay on a couple of the farm's horses and carts to transport people, just like we are doing for the ball. The children will love it.'

The moment the words were out of her mouth, she regretted her decision. Her stomach tightened and, too late, a vision of the chaos and extra work the fireworks would involve swam before her eyes.

Derek look visibly relieved, which made Flora feel a little better, but not much.

Mrs Honour almost smiled; her lips quivered while her eyes remained cold. Briskly, she stated, 'Excellent. It will be easy for you as you will be hosting the Lords and Ladies Ball shortly afterwards.'

Flora was at a loss to see how hosting a second major function a few days later made it easy for her to host the fireworks, but Mrs Honour had already moved on to another topic. 'What are you going to do about Draycott?'

'Draycott?' Derek seemed confused.

Flora's horticultural brain went instantly into full swing at the mention of the name. 'Paul Draycott is a total genius with his roses,' she said. 'He did frightfully well last summer at the village show. I must say, Derek, I do envy you having him as your gardener. My Mr Bert is a gem, but he is as old as the hills and—'

Mrs Honour was clearly as uninterested in Flora's problems with her gardener as she was in slippers and aspidistras. She cut across her as if she hadn't spoken. 'Really, the man needs locking up. He isn't safe. That temper of his is totally out of control.'

It was Flora's turn to look puzzled. 'I'm sorry, have I missed something? What has Paul Draycott got to do with – eh – the present situation?'

Mrs Honour gave Flora a withering look. 'If you spent more time contributing to the village you would have heard that just before Maud needed her appendix out, she was involved in an unfortunate incident. Maud hit Draycott's daughter Polly with her car.'

Flora gasped. 'She killed her?'

'No, just gave her a broken leg but Draycott made a frightful fuss about the whole thing. The man has never been quite right in the head since he came back from the war. He doesn't sleep or speak; he simply roams around the countryside all night.'

Flora immediate thought was, *If Maud hit my daughter, Debo, with her car, I would make a frightful fuss, too.*

Derek stared into the middle distance. 'I am afraid Draycott's distress was increased by Maud's behaviour after the accident. She was a bit offhand about it.'

Flora bit her tongue for a moment, then blurted out, 'That sounds like typical of Maud, running a child over then acting as if it's all too boring to deal with.'

Derek voice became wistful. 'I suppose at least I can re-employ him now. I didn't like dismissing him without a reference just before Christmas, but Maud insisted.'

Flora gasped, shocked that even Maud would insist on such a thing. Mrs Honour's tight-lipped expression suggested she agreed with Maud.

Derek swallowed before glancing up at the women. 'I suppose

that that at least is a good thing and it's good to know that the children's home will benefit from inheriting Maud's fortune.'

Mrs Honour sniffed. 'When I heard that Maud had left her not inconsiderable fortune to some children's home near Oxford, I thought it most odd.'

'So, Nanny was wrong,' mused Flora.

'What?' asked Mrs Honour sharply.

Flora gave a weak smile. 'Oh frightfully sorry, I was thinking out loud. Just something Nanny said on the drive over.' *Thank goodness I didn't actually articulate that we had the grieving widower down as the chief suspect motivated by Maud's money.* 'Children's home? Do tell me more. I didn't know Maud was interested in—' Flora just stopped herself from saying, *'in anyone but herself'*. Instead, she said, '—in a children's home.'

Privately, she thought, *Strange, I thought the only thing Maud disliked more than giving to charity was children.*

Derek's voice trailed away just as the housekeeper bustled in carrying a heavy tray ladened with goodies. She was still frowning with disapproval, especially when her eyes alighted on Flora.

'Now Derek, we must organise the funeral,' said Mrs Honour, her voice laced with glee.

Derek looked at her with horror.

'You don't need to do a thing,' she said. 'I will organise it all.'

Derek flinched. His mouth fell open and he raised a hand. 'No, no, I can—'

'So that's settled then. I believe I'm free on Thursday.'

'But that's only a few days away,' stammered Derek.

With a calm force, Mrs Honour stated, 'Far better to get it out of the way, especially with the fireworks, the ball and Christmas all to be got through in the next two weeks.'

'I'll do the flowers,' piped in Flora. Once more, she immediately regretted her offer. *When I'll have the time, goodness only knows.*

Mrs Honour frowned, she was evidently loath to relinquish any control but as she was hopeless at anything floral, she had little chance but to nod. Almost as if she was speaking to herself, she muttered, 'While I'm speaking to the vicar, I must tell him to stamp out these ridiculous stories about angels.'

'Angels?' queried Flora, baffled as to the link between, funerals, flowers and angels.

Mrs Honour sighed. 'So, you haven't heard the rumours? Several villagers are insisting that on the night Maud died, there were two beautiful, statuesque, blonde angels wondering around the village.'

'Goodness!' was all Flora managed to say before a knock at the door led to a muttered curse from Mrs Scrubs, before she reluctantly slunk away to open it.

Conversation in the drawing room stopped as all were curious as to who the new visitor was. Both Flora and Dorothy recognised Busby's steady baritone voice.

Flora felt a flutter of butterflies in her stomach, while Dorothy started to wag her tail enthusiastically.

Busby strode into the room, exuding professional confidence. His neat tweed suit and shiny shoes were in sharp orderly contrast to his unruly rusty-coloured curls and freckles. He lost no time in addressing Derek. 'Mr Adams, I am sorry to intrude at this sad time. Allow me to introduce myself, I am...' His hazel eyes alighted on Flora, ensconced on the sofa with Dorothy happily straining at her lead in her attempt to get closer to Busby. For a moment he seemed to forget his name as he blinked in amazement. Flora looked innocently up at him. He swallowed and with difficulty regained his composure. 'I am Chief Inspector Busby. I am afraid I need to ask you some questions.' He gave Flora a meaningful look. 'So if you ladies would kindly leave.'

The look he was giving Flora as he said these words was anything but kindly. She and Mrs Honour rose to their feet and Derek, ever the gentleman, mimicked their action.

Mrs Honour shook Derek's hand, saying in a loud voice that he was to contact her should he need anything and of course she would organise the funeral for him. Flora took advantage of this to approach Busby.

He glowered down at her. 'Mrs Farrington, I feel I must

caution you against meddling in police matters.' He raised one eyebrow. 'I just hope I have arrived here before you have had much time to create your habitual havoc.'

'I am shocked by your accusation, Inspector.' Flora stood as tall as her petite height would permit, her unruly brown curls framing her heart-shaped face, and blinked virtuously at the detective. 'When have I ever interfered in police matters?'

Busby regarded her with calm tawny eyes. With just a hint of a smile about his generous mouth, he replied, 'Well, the first time I am aware of was when you insisted we pretend to be a married couple at the Tews' Christmas house party. Then when we were in France, I lost count of the number of times you disrupted my investigation.'

'Details, details,' declared Flora, waving her hand in the air as if she could dismiss the notion away as easily as an errant wasp.

Busby returned to Derek Adams while Mrs Honour joined Flora in the hall. Mrs Scrubs seemed rather too delighted to show Flora and Mrs Honour the door. Nanny was already waiting there, her hat pinned to her head and her red carpetbag in hand.

Mrs Honour declared, 'I can't stand around here, I have work to do.' She strode away purposefully.

Flora felt a pang of pity for whoever was about to be the victim of Mrs Honour's work. *One knows any work that lady performs will be of the good work variety: charitable and condescending.* Out loud, she said, 'It's a shame I didn't get my cup of tea. Still, one can't have everything in life.' She turned to the housekeeper and asked, 'Could you kindly point out where Paul Draycott lives?'

Too late, she realised that this request might well provoke suspicion in this woman's mind but she need not have feared as Mrs Scrubs eyed her sharply. 'No doubt you'll be wanting to see if you can steal him away for your own garden. Word in the village is that your Mr Bert is past it. If you hold on a tick, I'll just grab my coat and show you. I have some bits to take them.'

True to her word she soon had her meagre coat wrapped around her even meaner figure and with a basket on her arm she led the way down the driveway.

Flora glanced at her watery eyes and cracked lips and struggled for a topic of conversation to break the silence. Her eyes alighted on the basket. 'Most kind of you to take pity on the Draycott family in their time of trouble.'

As she spoke an awful realisation struck her. *Goodness, I sound like a character in some highly moral Victorian novel – or, worse still, like Mrs Honour.* She shivered at the idea of her resembling Mrs Honour. *I need to read something racier. Perhaps something by Eleanor Glynn. How does the rhyme go? 'Would you like to sin with Eleanor Glynn on a tiger skin?'*

Mrs Scrubs' mind was obviously not on tiger skins, but sin did feature as she sniffed and tartly replied, 'I'm not doing it for the parents, I'm doing it for Betty. It ain't right for a child to be punished for the sins of her parents.'

There was a bitterness in her voice that made Flora ponder, *I wonder what sins Mrs Scrubs' parents committed that she was punished for as a child?*

Down the drive and on the edge of the village stood a small sandstone cottage. The cottage was in good order and even the garden gate swung neatly on its hinges – a sure sign of being well cared for.

'Here we are,' announced Mrs Scrubs.

Flora regarded the orderly garden, neatly put to bed for the winter. Everything was pristine, from the neatly mulched beds to sack-wrapped roses. 'Easy to see gardening is his passion as well as his profession.'

By the side of the cottage, a tall well-built man was chopping wood. Even from this distance it was easy to see that his right side was stiff and unyielding. Everyone in the village knew that he'd lost half his face as well as much of the use of his right side in the trenches. *Familiarity with veterans' more grisly war wounds softens the onlookers' horror – or perhaps one just gets better at masking one's horror,* mused Flora.

A small robin red breast was close by. Flora caught the tenderness with which this husk of humanity gently took something from his pocket and crumbled it on the ground for the bird. They were evidently used to working in tandem.

As Mrs Scrubs led the way, Paul looked up and glowered at the intruders.

'No need to scowl like that, Draycott; we're not here to see you, we're here for the babe,' commented Mrs Scrubs as she pushed past. She entered the back door with only a brief 'Cooey!' while Flora and Nanny followed.

The moment Flora entered the spotless kitchen, she felt as if she'd been wrapped in a comforting blanket of warmth. Coppers shone, the table gleamed with beeswax polish, a kettle sang on the hearth and the scent of baking was in the air. The festive season was much in evidence, with colourful paper chains strung across the low ceiling.

In front of the range, on a tartan rug, sat a small girl playing with a rag doll. Flora guessed her age to be about three and a half. She had a halo of golden ringlets and one of her little legs was stiffly encased in plaster.

As Flora crossed the threshold, a pretty young women, with buxom curves and the same golden curls, stopped singing, and smiled. 'Well, here's a treat and no mistake! Visitors!'

The toddler looked up and beamed. She had a delightfully open and innocent face.

'Come yourselves in and be welcome,' said the woman. 'This a joy and it's a blessing that I've just been baking.'

Mrs Scrubs sniffed yet again. 'I'm not stopping, some of us have work to do. I just came to leave this for Betty.' She took various foodie treats out of the basket and laid them on the side. 'Like as not, these fine folks have time enough to sit around and drink tea.' With that, she departed.

Mrs Draycott took advantage of the door being briefly open to call, 'Paul, come on in for your cup of tea.' She smiled at her guests. 'Sit yourselves down and I'll fetch the teapot and some buns.'

Flora was fond of children and chose the chair nearest to the little girl. She nodded towards the rag doll and politely enquired, 'Who is this?'

'She's Polly and I'm Betty.' The child looked quizzically at Flora with large blue eyes and held out the much-loved doll. 'Would you like a hold?'

'I certainly would!' Flora cradled the doll. 'I'm Mrs Farrington. Does your baby, Polly, sleep well?'

'Sleeps and eats like the angel she is,' declared the proud young mother, evidently repeating a phrase she had heard to describe herself. A large ginger tomcat strolled into the kitchen and laid himself down next to Betty. Sprawled out flat with just the occasional flick of his tail, he basked in the warmth of the range.

Sullenly Paul stomped in. He tossed an armful of small logs in the basket by the range and sat down at the table without making eye contact with either Flora or Nanny. Undeterred by her husband's rudeness, the young woman laughed. 'Oh Paul, will you leave off your sulking. We don't often have company.'

Without looking up, Paul muttered, 'Got work to do.'

Mrs Draycott gave Flora an apologetic smile. 'Now, I know from all the local flower shows that you be Mrs Farrington. It's many a fête I've seen you open in your fine clothes. I am Claire Draycott and this little bundle of joy is our Betty.'

Betty beamed. 'That lady already knows; we're friends.'

Once they were settled, Mrs Draycott poured the tea. Nanny surveyed the dark, inky liquid with satisfaction while Flora looked at it with trepidation and requested the milk. The buns were far more promising, glazed with sugar and smelling of cinnamon.

Mrs Draycott initiated the conversation. 'Now we are all sorted, perhaps, Mrs Farrington, you could be telling us what your business is with us?' She blinked her blue eyes at Flora.

*Oh dear why do I feel like a bit of a cad? How can I say, 'Gosh, Mrs Draycott these buns are delicious and, by the by, did your husband murder Maud?*

Fortunately, Flora was struck with inspiration. Remembering Mrs Honour had mentioned Paul Draycott was sacked, as well as Mrs Scrubs' suggestion that she wanted to see the Draycotts about a gardening job, she announced, 'I understand that Mr Draycott is currently – er – looking for a gardening position? I was wondering if he would care to come and work for me over at Farrington Hall?'

Mrs Claire Draycott's habitual smile exploded into a look of pure ecstasy. She clasped her hands together with excitement. 'Oh how wonderful! Do you hear that, Paul?'

Mr Draycott grunted but continued looking into his cup.

Claire Draycott's enthusiasm was short-lived. She bit her lip and a worry line showed between her brows as she mused, 'But then with Mrs Adams – gone – it could be that Mr Adams wants our Paul back.'

Flora was pleased that the conversation had turned to Maud's death and she eagerly leant a little forward saying, 'Yes, I did hear about the accident.' She glanced at Betty's leg in its cast, which left all to wonder if the accident she was referring to was Maud's death or Betty's broken leg.

Paul Draycott leapt to the conclusion that she was alluding to the latter and sprang to his feet, causing his chair to crash to the floor. 'It weren't no accident!' he yelled angrily. 'That woman drove like a maniac! Even after she hit our Betty, all the bitch could say was that she shouldn't have been on the road!' He spat on the ground, presumably to further express his contempt for Maud.

Claire was on her feet, speaking to him with the soothing tones a mother uses to calm an infant. 'There, now, don't take on so. No need to trouble yourself.'

Betty calmly continued to play with Polly; she was evidently used to these outbursts. Paul Draycott was trembling. Claire continued to murmur comfort into his ear.

Flora observed Claire's kindness as her own alarm at Paul's sudden outburst subsided. A tangled web of thoughts assailed her. *So, we've established that Paul Draycott has a murderous temper and that he hated Maud.* She looked at Betty, then at Claire. *But if we do prove that he is the killer, what will happen to these two innocents?*

She soon had more pressing things to worry about. There was a knock at the door, Claire went to answer it and led Busby into the kitchen.

Unsurprisingly, he looked none too pleased to see Flora having tea with his number one murder suspect. He cast her a furious look through narrowed eyes, but he addressed Mr and Mrs Draycott rather than her. He introduced himself and explained he need to ask them some questions, then he turned to Flora and Nanny. 'But first if you will please excuse me, I need to accompany these ladies to their car as I would like a word or two with them.'

Flora sprang hastily to her feet. 'No need, Inspector. Nanny and I will simply take ourselves off. Don't trouble yourself on our behalf; you just sit down and enjoy Mrs Draycott's excellent baking.'

'But I insist,' stated Busby through a taut mouth. He even went so far as to take Flora none too gently by the elbow and propel her to the garden gate, leaving Nanny to bid adieu and thank you to their hosts.

They were barely out of earshot before Busby swung her round to face him. His nostrils flared and the vein on his right temple pulsed. Flora had at times noticed that throbbing pulse whenever Busby was especially vexed with her, which was quite often.

'Mrs Farrington, I don't know what to say to you.'

Flora smiled. 'Then I suggest you remain silent and we will go.'

She turned to leave, pulling a reluctant Dorothy's lead.

But he caught hold of her hand, effectively stopping her and sending an annoying frisson of excitement through Flora's body. His hazel eyes were burning as he looked at her. 'Mrs Farrington, I will not tolerate your interfering in yet another case.'

Nanny whizzed up behind them. 'Quite, quite. Now if you'll stop your flirting, Inspector, Flora and I need to be getting home.'

Stunned, Busby abruptly dropped Flora's hand. 'I wasn't flirting,' he muttered defensively as the two ladies made haste to get in the car and depart.

As they drove out of the village Flora sighed. 'We didn't get a chance to ask Paul Draycott where he was at the time of Maud's demise.'

Huddled in her seat, Nanny said, 'Don't you worry about that, we can always go back and ask them some more questions. I've a mind to knit that little poppet a matinee jacket.'

# CHAPTER 2

### GALLONS OF TEA

Once home, Flora lit a fire in the library. Glancing out of the window, she thought, *This drizzle matches my mood: dreary. At least Lavinia will be here in a moment. And best of all Tony and Debo will be home for the holidays before supper time.*

She slipped off her shoes and curled up on the sofa in the library with Dorothy on her knee and the fire crackling in the fireplace. She had intended to re-read her copy of *The Inimitable Jeeves*, but in her current distracted state even such excellent literature failed to hold her attention. She glanced at her watch. Three o'clock. Her goddaughter Lavinia and her party would arrive soon. *And then I can have some cake.*

With a sighed, she patted Dorothy's head and that fine hound took it as an invitation to have her tummy tickled and rolled over. Flora laughed and obliged. Looking at Dorothy she commented, 'You don't have a care in the world, do you?'

Dorothy, with her eyes tightly shut, was just thinking, *I do hope you're not planning on spoiling a perfectly good tummy rub in front of the fire with one of your soul-searching monologues.*

That was exactly Flora's plan and she lost no time in beginning. 'I can't help feeling concerned about this whole Maud business. That poor man, Derek Adams. Honestly, Dorothy, if you'd seen him your heart would have broken.'

Dorothy squirmed on her back to get in a more comfortable position and thought, *I greatly doubt it – in fact unless the man had had a juicy beef bone he wanted to give me, I really shouldn't have cared a hoot about him.*

'If I can only work out who killed Maud, perhaps I can give the poor man a bit of resolution.'

Dorothy rolled her eyes. *Here we go!*

'The question is, who would have wanted to kill her and who had the opportunity?' She paused, stroking Dorothy's tummy while she contemplated this.

Dorothy wagged her tail and gave a low yap to remind Flora of her duties while thinking, *Who cares? Just focus, woman!*

'I need to find out more about that nurse, Susan Smythson. After all, Dr Honour seemed jolly worked up about her and those pills.' Flora glanced out of the window. The rain was still falling and a few golden leaves blew across the horizon. 'I hope Lavinia arrives before the storm properly starts up. I don't like the idea of her being on the road in bad conditions.'

*Again – don't care! Just tickle!*

Flora glanced at the fire and let her mind return to the Maud puzzle. 'Little Betty is so adorable.' She bit her lip and frowned. 'I dread to think what will happen to her if I do investigate and her father turns out to be the murderer.' She thought of his outburst. 'He certainly has a hair-trigger temper which doesn't bode well.' She sighed once more. 'Besides which, if he is the murderer I can hardly employ him as my gardener, which would be a tragedy – just think what he could do with my azaleas!' She paused. 'Nanny and I need to go back to the village and ask a few more questions – there can't only be the two suspects. I wonder who else has a temper and lives close by?' She gave Dorothy her full attention for a few moments before adding, 'And talking of tempers, I really do not care for the way Busby spoke to me.'

At the mention of Busby, Dorothy stiffened. *I will not hear a word spoken about my beloved Busby.*

She needn't have worried. Flora's attention span was sketchy at the best of times, but especially when she was in need of tea and cake. She looked at her watch again. 'Where is the child? I could really do with a cup of tea and a little something.'

As if by magic, the mere wish for a fortifying pot of tea was enough to conjure up Roberts, complete with the much-needed tea.

Flora smiled at the small, lithe man with his silver hair slicked back, and thanked the heavens that this excellent man had volunteered to act as her butler. For his part, he had decided to work for Flora more for the amusement factor than for the generous wage. Having met Flora the previous spring during a murderous adventure in France, he had decided she was highly, if unintentionally, amusing. Flora, for her part, found him an oasis of peace.

She glanced gratefully at him and he poured her a cup of the ever-blessed tea. 'Oh Roberts, I fear I have no idea who murdered Maud. The most likely suspect is a man called Draycott.'

'And you don't believe it was him?' enquired Roberts, with one beetling eyebrow raised.

Flora shook her head. 'It can't possibly be him.'

'Why not?'

'Well, for a start he is a simply amazing gardener, and he has the most adorable little daughter.'

Roberts regarded her with just the hint of a smile playing on his lips. 'Neither of those points would preclude him from committing murder.'

Flora sighed. 'I suppose you are right.' She took a sip of tea. 'But that's not my only worry.'

'Yes?'

'I've gone and landed us with hosting the fireworks party – but how are we to manage with the house full? The children will be here as well as Aunt Gigi and Lavinia.' She blew out a breath of exasperation. 'And we have the Lords and Ladies ball.'

He smiled. 'I presume Mrs Honour was involved in that.'

Flora nodded sadly.

He chuckled. 'She can be very forceful!'

'And I haven't had the courage to break the news to Mrs Wilkes yet. After all, a lot of the extra work will fall to her.'

'I wouldn't worry about her. She'll enjoy being outraged, followed by horrified and then she will revel in being a triumphant martyr as she manages everything with aplomb.' He beamed as he accurately described Mrs Wilkes' likely response, then his expression became more serious as a new thought struck him. 'But while we are on the subject of your staff; you do know that you employ a woefully inadequate number of people for a house this size?'

Flora shrugged. 'If I only I could get someone to help in the garden. Dear old Mr Bert is really getting beyond it.'

Roberts laughed. 'The garden is the least of your worries. Let's start with Mrs Wilkes – whoever heard of a house this size having just a house-keeper-come-cook? I have a lovely cousin in Bournemouth who has a boarding house only a fraction of the size of Farrington Hall and she has a lady who does double duties, but in a house like this you need far more help.'

Flora sniffed and a shade defensively said, 'Well, originally it was only meant to be temporary. Mrs Wilkes' sister was our cook for years and the two of them rubbed along as cook and housekeeper marvellously but then her sister was carried away in matrimony by the village butcher.' She gave him a confidential look. 'I did have my suspicions at the time as we suddenly started to have meat at every meal – bacon, chops and joints galore.'

'But to my understanding that was two years ago. Surely you could have found a replacement in that time?'

'I have tried, but every prospective replacement that I have suggested has been met with horror by Mrs Wilkes and threats of her giving notice.'

Roberts nodded. 'I can see your dilemma. What about the maid situation?'

'Mavis and Gladys are dears.'

'I agree but not exactly effective.'

'They may be really hopeless at cleaning but they are wonderfully happy to have about the house.'

'But you don't even have a lady's maid.'

Flora felt confident on this point and drew herself up in her sitting position. 'I can hardly be held responsible for my lady's maid running off to become a Crown Prince's Consort.' She turned her most radiant smile on Roberts. 'At least I have you.'

He raised an eyebrow once more. 'May I remind you that I'm not a real butler?'

'No, you are much better. How about you give me a hand working out who killed Maud?'

He merely chortled while taking his leave and added, 'My sleuthing days are over. If I wanted to catch criminals, I wouldn't have left my last employer.'

She had to wait a full hour and a half before Lavinia finally breezed in. She was dripping wet from the rain and – for some inexplicable reason – giggling. Flora blinked at her, perplexed. *Is the child wearing a cocktail dress? In this weather? At this time of day? Perhaps I should add some sensible wool vests to her Christmas presents.*

Lavinia's mass of short blonde curls shone in the firelight as did her lashings of scarlet lipstick. On her arm was a lizard of a youth whose name Flora did not quite catch, Biffy? Batty? Miffy? His hair was slicked back with an alarming amount of oil. His suit was of a garish colour and a striking cut. He was notably both pale and thin. His handshake was limp but at the same time clawing and Flora was not at all sure she cared for the intense way he looked at her. She extricated her hand as soon as possible.

She moved swiftly on to Lavinia and embraced her. 'Darling, I do hope the journey wasn't too frightful.'

'Not at all; we made it in record time,' said Lavinia blithely as she flopped down on the sofa next to Dorothy. The dachshund was delighted; she classified Lavinia as a gal who knew about tummy rubs.

Perplexed, Flora drew her eyebrows together. 'But you are so late?'

'Are we? No wonder I'm starving. Where's the cake?'

'Sandwiches first,' said Flora automatically. 'I'll just ring for tea to be brought in.'

She went to pull the rope by the fireplace. She was slightly surprised to find the lizard had followed her. He stood rather close, breathing over her shoulder. He brushed his hand over hers as he murmured, 'Allow me!'

Flora gave the rope a tug and sprang away from the reptilian chap. Feeling rather hot and flustered, her tone was crisp. 'I think I can manage, thank you.' She retreated to the vacant sofa. Lavinia and Dorothy were both sprawled out, dominating Flora's preferred sofa.

She risked a glance at the lizard. *Is he old enough to shave?* Evidently, he hadn't reached the age of discretion as he interpreted Flora's quelling look as an invitation to come hither. With a grin, he not only sat down on the same sofa as Flora but unnecessarily close to her. Flora shuffled a bit further away with the unpleasant thought, *Surely the child isn't trying to seduce me?*

The lizard shuffled too and gave Flora a significant look. She crossed her legs and turned her attention to Lavinia. 'Are you going on to a party?' she asked.

'No! Why do you ask?' asked Lavinia, innocently fluttering her wide blue eyes.

'Your dress.' Flora indicated the outfit that was both extremely short and embellished.

Lavinia looked down at it and laughed. 'Oh my! Godmother Flora, you really are as old as the hills. I suppose living down here in the sticks you really can't be expected to know about the latest trends.'

'I don't know about that!' said Flora tartly.

At the sound of a car on the gravel drive, Dorothy pricked up her ears and jumped off the sofa, running as fast as her short legs would take her to the front door. With no less enthusiasm Flora leapt to her feet and exclaimed, 'That must be the children home for the holidays. Excuse me.'

She reached the front door just as Debo burst through it. At ten, she was all arms and legs with short dark curls just like Flora's. Exuberantly she threw herself into her mother's arms exclaiming, 'Mummy darling! What fun! I hear there's been a murder and on our very doorstep, so to speak. Now I can have all the fun of sleuthing with you and Nanny. It was so rotten when you two were up to your eyeballs in dead bodies last spring and I was stuck in school.'

Tony was more reserved in his greeting. As he kissed Flora on the cheek she thought, *He grows more and more like his father. His blue eyes are exactly like Roger's and he even shares his way of speaking, not to mention his mannerisms.*

'Mother,' he said, 'I've been thinking about it and it's totally ridiculous for you to have to hire a chauffeur every time Debo or I need ferrying to or from school. Fortunately, the schools are so close that the obvious – the undeniably most sensible solution – is for you to get me my own car. Then—'

He broke off mid-sentence as Lavinia, in all her short-skirted beauty, strolled into the hall. She smiled at him. He stammered rather incoherently and turned a flaming pink. When she placed a languid hand on his shoulder and brushed his cheek with her lips while murmuring, 'Tony, how grown up you are,' Flora had a moment of concern that he would actually pass out.

Eventually, he managed to clear his throat and stammer, 'Rather! I was fourteen last birthday.'

Meanwhile, in the neighbouring village, Dr Honour had problems of his own to deal with.

His mother was looking at him over her porcelain teacup with her cool grey eyes. The scent of Earl Grey and lemon hung in the air. He disliked tea with his mother, partly because of the company but mainly because she maintained her unnaturally thin figure by foregoing sandwiches and cake.

'Victor, don't be difficult! You know as well as I do that Lady Robin Clarke is the perfect bride for you. She is sensible.'

Victor snorted. 'By sensible, you mean she has all the same views you have and has never read a book in her life. I cannot begin to imagine how dull life with her would be – she is hardly a blue-stocking.'

His mother shuddered. 'And thank goodness for that! If there's one thing I can't abide it's young women with opinions.'

She took a dainty sip of tea and sitting ramrod straight,

narrowed her eyes and in her most syrupy voice said, 'Need I remind you that your inheritance is entirely at my discretion. Just as well too, otherwise you would have squandered the lot of that ridiculous home for cowards.'

He clenched his fist and with a great effort kept his voice even. 'Not cowards mother: shellshocked heroes.'

'I am not prepared to discuss it anymore. Let's talk about village matters – did you see that frightful hat the vicar's wife wore on Sunday? Totally unsuitable, as I told her and the vicar. I am concerned about Mr Adams – he seems so low spirited.'

Victor sipped his tea; it was unpleasantly tart. He wished his mother would allow both sugar and milk in the house. 'What do you expect? The man's just lost his wife.'

'Can't you give him a tonic of some sort to buck him up?'

'As I have told you before, there is such a thing as doctor-patient confidentiality, and I am not at liberty to discuss my patients with you,' said Victor wearily.

'Speaking of Mr Adams, I plan on going there tomorrow. Such as scandal – would you believe that chit of a girl, Smythson is still staying there and without a chaperone? I know about women like that. If I don't put a stop to it, that hussy will have her claws in him. Men are so easily swayed.'

Victor sighed. 'I wish you wouldn't.' Then a thought struck him. 'Smythson?' he mused. 'It's an unusual name – didn't you have some business connection with a Smythson?'

Suddenly his mother seemed totally uninterested in tea and conversation, and glanced at her watch. 'Now I know you have leisure time to spare, but I really must get on.' With that she rose. 'You can see yourself out, can't you?'

Mrs Scrubs, the housekeeper, had taken her cup of tea to the privacy of her bedroom. Her cat wound in and out of her legs purring, while her mistress muttered, 'At least now Maud Adams has gone, my secret is safe.'

She unpinned her tight bun and a surprising cascade of luxuriant hair tumbled down her back. She thought of her grandmother's words when she'd been fourteen. 'It's your mark of shame – keep it hidden, my girl!'

And she had.

In the same house, Nurse Susan Smythson was pottering in the drawing room. She picked up Derek's sweater which he had left on the arm of the sofa. Carefully she folded it and paused, thinking, *How could such a fine man be married to someone like Maud?* She thought of the old saying, 'Bad blood will out.' *How true it was in Maud's case. She was just as wicked as her father before her.* Her own father came to mind, kind, generous, honourable, and she bit back a tear. *And look at where all his nobility got him.* She straightened her spine. *At least with Maud gone, perhaps there is some hope for me.*

In the Draycott's cottage not far away, Claire was thinking much the same thing. She watched Paul and Betty laughing as they played together on the rug in front of the range and smiled. *Perhaps now that Maud Adams is dead, this is how our lives can be.*

# CHAPTER 3

*THE FUNERAL*

The day of the funeral arrived in the blink of an eye. 'Is it wrong, Nanny dear, that I am rather looking forward to today?' Flora could barely keep the glee out of her voice.

Nanny clamped a podgy hand more firmly on her stiff black hat. It was in danger of being carried away as Flora sped her red two-seater Morgan around a corner.

'Yes! Utterly shameless and reprehensible to be elated when on the way to a funeral, but I wouldn't expect anything less from you,' stated Nanny firmly.

The first fat drop of rain fell, landing on Nanny's nose. As one hand was occupied holding down her hat and the other hand was securing her large red carpetbag on her lap she couldn't wipe it away, so instead she sourly pointed out, 'What is ridiculous is you insisting on us going to the funeral in this sardine can of a car. We are about to be drenched.'

'Nonsense, Nanny, it's just a drop. Can't we just call it professional curiosity?' Flora slowed down as she overtook a boy on a bicycle.

'Uh. Since when did you join the police force?' Flora glanced over at her and Nanny shrieked, 'Eyes on the road!'

Flora obliged while responding, 'Well I am sort of an unofficial police helper and what better way to find out who committed Maud's murder than by being front and centre at her funeral? Absolutely anyone who has read a single murder mystery knows the killer always shows up at the funeral.'

'Good to know,' muttered Nanny. 'Shrewd move on your part

to offer to do the flowers at Derek Adams' house. After all, the man will want it looking presentable for the wake.'

Flora grinned. 'And it's the one thing that old busybody, Mrs Honour, is hopeless at, so she could hardly decline. I gather she has taken charge of everything else. I had dear old Mr Bert drop off my scissors and some foliage from the garden earlier so they should be waiting for me in the flower room.' She frowned. 'Do modern houses have flower rooms?'

Nanny shrugged. 'Can't say I know or care.'

As they arrived within sight of Derek's house, Flora sighed. 'I don't think the austerity of this place is growing on me with familiarity. There are just too many sharp angles.'

'Can't say I care for it much either,' agreed Nanny.

Flora parked her car discretely to one side. She leapt nimbly from her seat and smoothed down her black dress and light overcoat. She checked her cloche hat was still firmly on her head and then she went around the car to help Nanny lever herself out.

'Here you go, old bean,' she said as Nanny's bulk eased out. She surveyed Nanny's customary garb. 'You may dress as if you don't know that Queen Victoria is dead but your habit of always wearing black comes in handy for funerals.'

Nanny grunted a good-natured, 'Less of your cheek, my girl.'

As they walked towards the house, Flora regarded the black ribboned wreath on the front door. 'As I'm here to do the flowers, I guess we'd better go around to the back door.'

'Quite, and we are also more likely to be able to sneak up on the inhabitants and overhear Miss Smythson and the housekeeper, Mrs Scrubs, confessing to Derek that they jointly committed the murder,' commented Nanny dryly as she creaked across the gravel.

They walked down the side of the house and almost immediately spotted Mrs Scrubs, not in the act of confessing but pausing with a heavy coal bucket in her hands, presumably to stock the range. Thin and taut, she was an unwelcoming figure. Her lips were drawn together in her characteristic scowl. She bobbed her head up and down. *Just like my pet tortoise,* mused Flora. A large ginger tom sidled up to her, mewing. Before their eyes, she transformed into a beaming and affectionate cat owner.

'There you are, my darling Ginger,' she crooned, bending over to lovingly stroke the cat as he wound around her sparrow-slim legs. 'You'd better keep out of the way today – the house will be full but I'll put some goodies on one side for you.'

She straightened and saw Nanny and Flora. Instantly the scowl returned and her eyes narrowed. 'You be here to do the flowers.'

'That's right, Mrs Scrubs,' beamed Flora, striding past the woman and into the house. The flowers were on the kitchen table so that answered the flower room question. Flora regarded them and told herself firmly, *Focus on the flowers and don't think about this table being the location for Maud's appendix operation.*

Nanny had no such qualms. 'Did you have much scrubbing to do after Mrs Adams' op?' she enquired brightly, nodding toward the table.

'Let me tell you…'

Flora could only be grateful that Nanny and Mrs Scrubs were only passing through the kitchen on the way to lay the fire in the drawing room. *I'm not sure how many gory details of the operation I can stomach.*

This left Flora alone with the flowers and in a prime position to view the back garden. The click of the gate made her look up. *I say, here comes Mrs Honour and her son.* Flora noted that older woman's black costume was exquisitely cut, but of more interest to her was the angry expression marring Mrs Honour's normally demure face. *Goodness, they are not a happy pair,* thought Flora as she took in the way the man glowered at the ground, avoiding his mother's eyes.

They were soon close enough for Flora to hear what Mrs Honour was saying. 'Really, Victor, I will not hear another word. Lady Robin Clarke is coming for the weekend and I expect you to spend the entire time entertaining her. It's ridiculous you think seeing patients should take precedence.'

Flora could see a flicker of annoyance cross his face. The sharp line of his jaw was emphasised as he clenched his teeth and jutted his chin out but he did not reply. At this point they reached the threshold of the back door. Both coloured as they realised the whole exchange had been heard by Flora.

Dr Honour uttered a dignified, 'Excuse me, Mrs Farrington, I will just go and check on Derek.'

Mrs Honour rapidly recovered her composure but clearly felt some explanation was required. She fixed Flora with her granite eyes and stated, 'The young need a steady hand to guide them.'

Surprised Flora exclaimed without thinking, 'But surely he's over thirty!'

Mrs Honour gave Flora an age-assessing look, before crisply saying, 'Exactly! Now if you will excuse me, there are a million thing to be done.' She whisked past Flora, and into the house with her head held high.

Flora returned to her task. She had selected a tall, elegantly tapered vase. *Not very stable, but there shouldn't be any drunken revellers at a funeral who might knock it over.* She arranged some dried opaque honesty in the vase which she paired with some sprays of artificial red berries and some ever-green foliage.

She stood back to admire it. *I would really like to add a few ostrich feathers but that would hardly be funeral-appropriate. Still, it should brighten up Derek Adams' rather nondescript hallway.*

Carefully, she carried it into the hall and placed it on a mat on a round table, directly in front of the front door. She took a moment to angle it, to show it off to its best advantage.

Nanny and Mrs Scrubs bustled past from the drawing room, coal bucket empty and chatting hard. 'You are quite right, Mrs Scrubs; we should get a spare clothes hanger or two from upstairs – folk are bound to want to take their coats off.'

'Though I can't think there will be that many. After all, it wasn't as if Mrs Adams had any family, much less friends,' added Mrs Scrubs in a matter-of-fact tone as she began to climb the staircase. 'Of course, your English funerals are poor stuff when compared to the Irish wakes of my homeland.'

'And don't I know it! I grew up in Ireland.'

'You did? I thought you said you grew up in Cumbria?'

Flora heard no more as they disappeared upstairs. She was about to return to the kitchen and the remaining flowers when a raised voice stopped her. Automatically she looked towards the open door to the drawing room where she could clearly hear Mrs Honour. Flora knew the polite thing to do would be to quietly withdraw but naturally she had no intention of doing that. Silently she moved towards the door, all the better to both hear and, with any luck, see whatever was going on.

Miss Smythson stood before both the fire and Mrs Honour, who was holding forth. She stood very erect, thin and wiry without even the smallest hint of warmth about her. *Goodness, that metal poker by the fireplace shows more humanity than Mrs Honour in this moment.* 'Now, Miss Smythson, it really would be better for you and all concerned if you left straight after the funeral.'

Miss Smythson calmly looked Mrs Honour in the eye and with great self-possession replied, 'Mr Adams has asked that I stay on, at least until he is back from the little holiday he is about to take.'

Mrs Honour deliberately ran her cold eyes over the younger woman, starting with her head and finishing with her well-polished toe. She took a step back and crossed her arms. With menace, she hissed, 'There are things about your background you would not wish to come out.'

Nurse Smythson's apple cheeks paled and her voice faltered. 'You have no right..'

Mrs Honour pressed on, 'I imagine that you really would not want a little birdie to tell the police – especially in light of Mrs Adams' demise.'

Her work done, Mrs Honour stalked out of the drawing room via the opposite door. Nurse Smythson stood unnaturally still for a moment before she began to sway.

Recognising the signs of an imminent swoon, Flora rushed forward, only to overtaken by Dr Honour. *He must have been listening to it all just behind me! A sneaky, sleuthing medic?*

Dr Honour caught Nurse Smythson in his arms and carefully led her to the sofa. She came to and sprang back from the doctor's grasp. The colour had not returned to her cheek before she attempted to stand up. Dr Honour put a restraining hand on her arm, only to have it shaken off.

'Nurse Smythson, I must insist that you rest a while,' he said in a very authoritarian doctor's voice.

Nurse Smythson stared angrily at him. 'Dr Honour, as you are neither my employer nor my superior in this setting you have absolutely no right to tell me what to do.' She stood unsteadily, all the while glowering at Dr Honour with defiance.

The looks the pair were exchanging were enough to set Flora's thoughts spiralling. *Goodness! Talk about sizzling chemistry!* The chime of a distant clock snapped her back to business rather than romance. *But enough of that. I need to finish off the flowers before we have to leave for the funeral.*

Eventually they formed a sad little funeral party. With their umbrellas up they trailed to the church where the bell tolled a sad lament.

Derek was supported on either side by Dr Honour and Nurse Smythson. He shuffled rather than walked. His gaze was vacant. His eyes seemed to have sunk into his hollow face. Flora felt she finally understood that trite description of someone being a shell of a man.

She was dismayed to find that there were no smart cars lined up by the church. When they entered the church there were no mourners, just a vague smell of dust and incense, and a coffin with expensive hothouse flowers on top.

Flora gazed around the church, at the polished wooden pews, all of which were sadly empty. By the altar with its golden cross, a few white lilies blended their scent with the chilly air and offered a hint of serenity. The high, vaulted ceiling added to the sense of peace as did the dappled light streaming in from the stained glass windows.

Flora was surprised – or maybe disappointed – that Busby was not present. It was the only funeral she had ever been to where there were almost more pallbearers to carry the coffin than there were mourners. *I knew old Maud wasn't exactly little Miss Popular but this...* She took a seat in an empty pew near the front of the church, uncomfortably close to the coffin. She wished she could have sat discreetly at the back of the church with Nanny and Mrs Scrubs.

The vicar's wife was there in what Mrs Honour would deem another unsuitable hat. As Flora sat on her uncomfortable pew, her mind wandered. *There were a few Christmas cards on display at the Adams' home. Surely if someone has gone to the trouble to write a Christmas card* – she thought of her own sizeable pile of unwritten cards and amended her thought – *the not inconsiderable effort to write a card, they would have also made time to come to the funeral?*

The vicar valiantly rushed through the service. They struggled to sing 'Abide with Me' accompanied by a wheezing organ. Flora found the whole experience so depressing she felt relieved when it was time to proceed out of the church behind the coffin.

Once outside, she took in a deep breath of fresh air and held her face up to a ray of sun that peeked out briefly between heavy black clouds. Various villagers were lined up against the low stone wall that surrounded the graveyard. Among them Flora spotted the two boys who had found Maud's body. For a moment she wondered why they weren't at school, then she recalled it was the school holidays. Paul Draycott stood out – despite his war injuries he was still a tall, imposing figure. His set expression was hard to read. Flora's chief thought was, *At least there are a few more people to see Maud off.*

Her attention quickly reverted to Derek. He had noticed the freshly-turned earth around the grave which was to be his wife's final resting place. He stopped walking suddenly and stared at the open wound in the grass. He probably would have dropped to the ground had Nurse Smythson and Dr Honour not grabbed an elbow each to support him.

He seemed to brace up and by the time they were at the graveside he was able to stand alone. The vicar intoned the last few words of the funeral service and Derek shuffled forwards to throw his handful of earth on the coffin. He dashed a tear off his sunken cheek. The funeral drew to its natural close.

Flora looked at the tiny funeral party and wondered, *Who is going to eat all the food that has been prepared for the reception? Even I have a limit of how much I can wolf down at one sitting!*

The drizzle was turning to rain. Prompted by Nurse Smythson, Derek reluctantly tore himself away from the graveside. Slowly he began to walk back to the house followed by the small band of supporters.

It was at this moment that, out of the corner of her eye, Flora spotted Busby. He was flanked by two uniformed bobbies and they were walking with purpose. She looked from Busby to Paul Draycott. Her pulse quickened and her thoughts whirled. *Surely not? They can't be here to arrest Paul Draycott, can they? Surely the only thing they have against him is his fight with Maud just before her demise? They can't take him away just before Christmas too?* She experienced a sinking feeling in the pit of her stomach and her thoughts went straight to his wife, Claire, and their adorable daughter, Betty. *How will they cope if he is arrested?* She swallowed. *Or, heaven forbid, if he's hung for Maud's murder?*

Paul had seen them, too. His eyes grew huge, animal-like in their terror. He turned to run, but not quickly enough as the two bobbies seized him.

*Oh no!* thought Flora as she hurried over. Dr Honour had evidently also observed the scene and like Flora he silently peeled away from the sad group heading back to the house. His mother tried to place a restraining hand on his arm but he easily shook her off.

By the time Flora reached Paul, the cornered man was breathing heavily and his limbs were visibly trembling. There was a sheen of sweat on his forehead. The two boys were watching with ill-hidden excitement.

Flora swallowed again, trying to calm herself. Her eyes felt hot. 'Busby, you can't do this. Think of his wife and child.'

Busby had a pinched expression around his eyes. He clenched his jaw. With a sharp tone he snapped, 'I am thinking of them; that is why we are doing this here and not at his home.' He instantly regretted his harsh tone and his look softened. 'Mrs Farrington, Flora, let's talk about this later.'

But it was too late. Flora was furious and in no mood to be placated. She threw him a venomous look.

Dr Honour was far less combative than Flora. He stood before Busby with his arms slightly open and outstretched. He tilted his head and gave Busby strong eye contact. 'Inspector, I understand you have a job to do. Perhaps I could be of assistance.'

Paul started to struggle and at a nod from Busby they began to manhandle him towards the nearby police van.

Dr Honour's voice took on a new urgency. 'Is this really necessary? As his doctor, I feel that confining Mr Draycott in a close space surrounded by men in uniform is the worst thing that could happen to him.'

He did not mention the war, the forced claustrophobia of the trenches with uniformed officers barking orders that sent men to their deaths.

Busby understood and nodded. Quietly he said, 'Would you be able to accompany him to the station?'

Flora's mind was in a whirl. *I may not be able to stop this ridiculous arrest but I can do what I can for Claire and Betty.*

By the time the police and Dr Honour managed to get a struggling Paul into the car, Flora was already striding to the Draycott cottage. She was not totally certain what she was going to do or say when she got there but she was determined that Claire and Betty should know that they were not alone.

She reached the cottage in record time, knocked briefly on the back door and when Claire gave a cheerful, 'Come in – it's open,' she walked in.

As before, the kitchen was warm and welcoming. Mother and daughter were at the kitchen table, midway through a riotous game of Snap. Both gave Flora wonderful smiles. Betty even squealed in delight.

Claire was the first to realise from Flora's expression that something was wrong. Flora's mouth was dry and the lump in her throat momentarily stopped her from speaking.

'What is it?' stammered Claire.

Flora felt a sharp pain in her chest. Her throat was still tight and she had difficulty swallowing but she managed to say, 'I am very sorry, but I have some very bad news. I am afraid Paul has been arrested for the murder of Maud Adams.'

Claire froze; she was totally immobile. All the colour drained from her face. Confused, Betty looked from Flora to her mother then her lower lip quivered, and she reached her arms out to her mother with a pitiful sob.

Flora hastened to throw her arms round both of them. Claire shook her head, repeatedly murmuring, 'No, no, no.'

'I will engage the best possible legal help.' Then with the same impulsive nature that saw her doing the flowers for the funeral and hosting the fireworks party, Flora squeezed them both and declared, 'I promise that I will find the real killer and you shall have Paul safely home for Christmas.'

It was nearly midnight when Busby got home that night. He was tired – not with the natural tiredness of a day well spent but with the crushing weariness of a man who feels defeated by his life. *Thank goodness Dr Honour was there,* Busby contemplated, as he took off his shoes and loosened his tie. Dr Honour hadn't liked the business any more than Busby had but they both knew they had a duty to perform. Dr Honour had sat quietly by Paul as Busby attempted to question him. *Ridiculous trying to question a man who was either staring into space or twitching uncontrollably* thought Busby bitterly. It was a relief when they could call it a day and Dr Honour had been able to inject Paul with something strong enough to send him into oblivion, at least for a few hours. Busby rather wished the doctor had given him a sedative too, tired as he was, he knew he was too keyed up to sleep. Busby thought of Paul in his prison cell. One comfort was that he did not need to tell the night constable to be gentle with the prisoner; the elderly constable had lost two sons to the war and would be compassionate.

'Don't be too hard on yourself.' Dr Honour had said, as he got in his car to leave. 'You really didn't have a choice but to bring him in and question him – he is such an obvious person of interest in the case.'

Busby had looked at him and stated, 'There are days when I hate my job.'

Dr Honour had given a weak smile and said, 'Me too.'

Busby couldn't be bothered to make himself a cup of tea. He sat staring into space before slowly formulating a plan. *Tomorrow, I will have my men do house to house questioning in the village and I can talk with Paul again.* Even in his mind he avoided using the word, 'questioning'. *If there is no concrete evidence against the man, I will be quite within my rights to release him.*

The thought of being able to legitimately free Paul brought a smile to his face but it was soon superseded by a scowl as he recalled Flora, all outraged passion and fury.

'That woman!' He muttered out loud. He allowed himself to feel anger, *Its all very well for her to go around full of moral outrage but I have to follow the letter of the law.*

He exhaled. *The best thing I can do for Paul is to follow methodical police practice. I will make some phone calls and find out some more about the people living in the same house as Maud.* He sighed, *It was so much easier when people didn't move around so much. Mrs Scrubs, Derek Adams, Nurse Smythson and Maud herself are all new to the village so finding out more about them will mean hours on the phone.* Thinking about ringing Somerset House and checking details of birth certificates and the like, not to mention the 1921 census did nothing to lift his spirits. With a sigh he decided he would make himself a cup of tea after all.

# CHAPTER 4

## *FIREWORK PREPARATIONS*

'Heaven must be like this!' declared Flora to her uninterested dachshund, Dorothy. Enveloped in sumptuous silk pyjamas, propped up by a generous number of pillows and covered with a luxurious eiderdown, Flora was content. Shameful though it was, a good night's sleep went a long way towards softening her overwrought emotions after the funeral.

She sipped her excellent black coffee. Hot, strong and rich, it was all that she could dream of. 'I can forgive Mrs Wilkes many a soggy roly-poly pudding as long as she continues to start my day with a cup of bliss.'

A bountiful number of bare branches adorned the vase at the foot of her four-poster bed. Flora had jazzed the arrangement up with the few red berries she had managed to find.

As she regarded the display she mused, 'Why is every bush awash with festively red berries in autumn, only to be all gone come Christmas, when one really wants them to brighten up the halls?' She sighed as a charitable thought stuck her. 'I suppose at least the birds enjoy eating them.'

Dorothy was not a morning person. She gave a doggy sigh. *Why does she have to be such a lark? Doesn't the woman know it's still sleeping time?* She firmly shut her eyes. *I do hope she stops talking soon.* In the night, Dorothy had managed to migrate from her basket to under Flora's covers. To the her great delight, the eiderdown blocked out all of the morning light and dulled much of Flora's monologue.

While Dorothy snuggled down, enjoying the warmth of the

bed, Flora gazed out of the window at the blue sky and the stark branches of the trees.

'At least it looks dry for the fireworks tonight. What a lovely day for a walk. Would you like to walk down to the hall this morning when I pop in to help with the preparations in the hall?' At the mention of one of her favourite words – 'walk' – Dorothy lazily wagged her tail. 'I can't believe it's the fireworks already, it's almost time for our ball and then Christmas will be here before we know it.' Flora took a long, unhappy sip of coffee, 'Time is marching on and I am no further along in working out who is responsible for Maud's murder. I haven't seen Busby since that awful funeral.' Dorothy recognised another favourite word – 'Busby' – and once more wagged her tail. 'I wonder if he's still furious with me?'

She poured herself another cup of coffee before continuing, 'Derek Adams was so devastated at the funeral – he seemed the only person who was in the slightest bit downcast by Maud's demise. Sad that Maud had so few friends. I would like to think there would be a tear or two shed as my coffin was lowered in the ground. It would be gratifying if there was at least a bit of wailing and gnashing of teeth.'

At this point in her musings, Nanny bustled in. Flora smiled warmly. 'Ah, Nanny, would you cry buckets at my funeral?'

'Oceans, dear, but more importantly what are you doing still in bed? There is work to be done! You need to get up and get yourself downstairs and outside before that son of yours causes an explosion. I caught him pouring petrol on the bonfire in order to make sure we had a really good blaze. And when I left, he was explaining to Debo that if they added a bit more gunpowder to the fireworks they would really go off with a pop.'

Flora was far too used to Tony's adventures to be overly alarmed and just murmured, 'Bless the child' before taking another sip of coffee.

The bed creaked as Nanny flopped her enormous bulk onto it. Her sensible black boots swung above the floor. With her small twinkling eyes she regarded Flora. 'You do need to get up. Apart from curbing Tony's enthusiasm, half the village is in the kitchen preparing food for tonight and the other half is in the orchard prepping the bonfire and fireworks.'

Flora squinted at her neat little travel clock on her bedside table. 'What? It's only ten o'clock.'

'Precisely – high time you were up! Besides, I've been thinking, my girl. You've been slacking.'

'Nanny! Me? Slacking? Never!' expostulated Flora indignantly. After that exertion she relaxed back into the luxurious comfort of her bedcovers and with a lazy smile purred, 'Well, only on occasion.'

Nanny shook her head, causing a small shower of hairpins to cascade on to the eiderdown. 'Here we are, days after Maud's death and we are no further forward discovering who did her in. All the village will be at the fireworks tonight and the murderer is bound to be there, so all we have to do is keep our wits about us and ask the right questions.'

'I do admire your optimism, old bean, but I seem to recall you saying exactly the same thing before the funeral. As to us being not getting anywhere nearer to finding the murderer – that is just what I've been lamenting to Dorothy.'

Nanny glanced at the small lump under the covers. 'That poor dog. We really do need to get you spending more time with Busby and less time talking to your mutt.' Dorothy was only half listening but wagged her tail at the mention of her beloved, Busby. 'I suggest you and Dorothy get up. You can quickly do your duty by smiling and nodding at all the village worthies beavering away getting everything ready before getting yourself outside for a walk. The exercise will do you both good.'

'Excellent idea,' declared Flora, scrambling out of bed.

Nanny departed and Flora dressed quickly in a sensible tweed skirt and cashmere twinset, all in a shade of golden brown.

When Flora and Dorothy got downstairs the kitchen appeared to be crammed full of at least three quarters of the village. Flora could hear her own Mrs Wilkes and the fearsome Mrs Honour, shouting out commands, leading her to think, *Best leave them to it.*

She went to the boot room and pulled on her warm coat and gumboots. She wrapped around her neck the bright red scarf that Nanny had knitted for her last Christmas.

As ever, Nanny was right; the walk was heavenly. There was just enough crispness in the air to be refreshing. Weak sunshine glimmered through the dark branches of the majestic beach tree. Flora inhaled deeply. 'I do adore the woody scent of winter.'

Dorothy's nose was firmly clamped to the ground as she muttered, *Tell me about it!*

They were just returning home when Flora was surprised to meet Paul with Claire and Betty. *How wonderful! Busby must have released Paul.* Thus, with a 'throw-away' thought, Flora dismissed Busby's careful questioning of Paul and his men's door to door inquiries in the village. All of which had resulted in Busby's conclusion that there was no hard evidence against Paul.

Both mother and daughter were laughing.

Betty was being pushed along by her father in a wheelbarrow as a makeshift wheelchair. Her leg was safely propped up and she had a mountain of rugs and cushions to keep her comfy and warm.

Claire was carrying a basket of russet apples as the Draycott family's contribution to the upcoming feast. Her pretty face lit up in a beaming smile and her eyes sparkled as she greeted Flora. 'Mrs Farrington! Thank you so much – as you can see, the police have let our Paul out. I bet it was your doing.'

Flora demurred, 'I'm delighted to see it, but I really can take no credit for it. I expect they just wanted to ask a question or two?' She raised an inquisitive eyebrow and was looking intently at Paul, thinking *Ooh, I do hope he says something about why he was released and at the same time drop a clue about what the police know,* but he just looked morosely in front of him. She tried a different tack. 'Those apples look magnificent, far better than any of mine. Perhaps after the harvest supper is out of the way we could resume our conversation about you coming to work for me?'

He gave a noncommittal grunt with which she had to be satisfied. Claire gave her an apologetic smile.

Cheerfully Flora announced, 'I believe Mrs Honour has allocated a place for all delicious food offerings.' She led the way into her home. Mrs Honour was nowhere to be found in the hubbub of the kitchen. Flora left the Draycotts in Nanny's capable hands and started to make her way to the boot room to shed her coat and boots.

Through the doorway, she was surprised to find that, far from commanding affairs in the kitchen, Mrs Honour was closeted in the boot room, and she was not alone. Nurse Smythson had evidently just walked in. Quickly, Flora stepped back, keen not to be seen, while she shamelessly eavesdropped.

Mrs Honour did not notice Flora, partly because of her swift actions but largely because all her attention was directed towards the young nurse. With narrowed eyes and her arms folded in front of her meagre chest, she regarded the other woman. Stiffly, in a quiet unfriendly tone, she stated, 'Oh! Nurse Smythson, I didn't expect to see you here.'

Nurse Smythson seemed to draw herself up to her full height and looking Mrs Honour in the eye, bestowed on her a none too warm smile. 'I am always happy to help with village activities.'

Mrs Honour gave a dismissive sniff. 'That's as maybe.' Her cold eyes took on a glacial glint. 'How long are you planning on staying in the village? With Mrs Adams gone, you have no job here as such.' Her voice lowered to almost a hiss. 'I thought I'd made myself quite clear when we had our little chat that it would be better if you took up residence elsewhere.'

Calmly Nurse Smythson replied, 'Yes, you made yourself quite clear.'

There was a silence. Flora held her breath, wondering who would blink first.

Mrs Honour swallowed. 'But you are still here.'

With a lack of emotion and an economy of words that Flora could only dream of, Nurse Smythson said, 'Yes.'

Flora thought she detected a pulse rising on Mrs Honour's temple and her voice rose an octave when she said with emphasis, 'And yet you are *still* here?'

Flora's admiration for Nurse Smythson was growing by the second. Still in total control, the nurse explained, 'You made your position very clear, but whatever your thoughts may be on the subject it has absolutely no impact on what I may choose to do.'

There was another deafening silence, and the two women eyed each other with such menace that Flora felt it would be an act of charity to intervene.

'What-oh!' she exclaimed brightly, as she entered the room. Thinking as she did so, *I must stop reading so much PG Wodehouse.*

Both Mrs Honour and Nurse Smythson turned their attention to her.

*At least they are united in their distaste for me!* thought Flora, smiling.

Mrs Honour utilised her greater height to look down her elegant nose at Flora. A slight flare of the nostrils indicated her disapproval of her interruption. With great dignity and a distinct lack of affection she addressed her. 'Excuse me for a moment, Mrs Farrington.' She now turned to Nurse Smythson. Flora was impressed to note that Mrs Honour's tone had been imbued with balmy Mediterranean warmth when she spoke to Flora, compared to the timbre deployed on Nurse Smythson. 'Nurse Smythson, since you are here you can move and put up those trestle tables in the orchard.'

Mrs Honour indicated an intimidating pile of heavy folded tables that were stacked in the corner.

Flora looked from the tables to Nurse Smythson and automatically said, 'Oh I say, that's a job and a half! I'll just secure Dorothy and then I'll give you a hand. Or better still, let's get some strapping chap to do it.'

Mrs Honour was having none of it. Rigid in stance and calm in voice she firmly stated, 'I am sure Nurse Smythson is more than capable of moving a few tables. Your skills, Mrs Farrington, are required for buttering the bread.'

Without missing a beat she surprised Flora by grasping her elbow and propelling her towards the kitchen table, where there was a mountain of loaves and a smaller hill of butter. Flora, was fairly certain that any competent six-year-old in the village would make a better job of cutting the bread into slices and buttering it than she would, but Mrs Honour was not the sort of person one said no to. *If only I possessed a haughty air that could squash a village autocrat with a single stare, I wouldn't be lumbered with the bread and butter.*

Flora tried to send Nurse Smythson a sympathetic look and noticed that Dr Honour standing just behind the young nurse. His jaw was clenched, his eyes narrowed and the look he gave his mother was one of pure dislike. *He clearly doesn't approve of his mother's behaviour any more than I do.* Flora caught a distinct change in his expression as he turned his gaze on Nurse Smythson. *That isn't a look of pity. I say, do I direct a glimmer of admiration? Goodness me, I can't wait to finish buttering my bread and to fill Nanny in. Her Irish heart always loves a bit of romance, especially when it involves star-crossed lovers.*

Flora looped Dorothy's lead around a nearby chair and put on a heavy green apron. Out of the corner of her eye she noticed the nurse start to lift the table. *Gosh! That Nurse Smythson is less of a helpless maiden and more of an Amazon.*

Flora had haphazardly cut a thick slice of bread when she saw Nurse Smythson stagger under the cumbersome weight of the table. She was not the only person to notice. Dr Honour was walking past carrying a ladder. Before he could put the ladder down and come to her rescue, Derek Adams appeared from nowhere.

Flora was surprised by the energy in his movements. *Now there's a chap who has bounced back quickly. He hardly looks like the same man who was at the funeral.*

He beamed at Nurse Smythson as he took the end of the table. *Do I detect a twinkle in his eye?* The pair of happy helpers made eye contact and Miss Smythson's face lit up, making Flora ponder, *I wonder how old she is? I'd put her down as a matron of mature years but right now she looks quite youthful.*

Dr Honour, plus ladder, strode past, scowling.

'Mrs Farrington, did you hear me?' demanded Mrs Honour.

'Yes,' she murmured none too honestly as she returned to her buttering, but not for long. As soon as she had a few slices on a plate she threw a tea towel over the top and planned her escape. *I feel almost anything would be more enjoyable than this!* She gave Dorothy a look that she hoped conveyed, *Come on Dorothy, let's flee while Mrs Honour's back is turned.*

They hurried out, only pausing briefly in order for Flora to pull on her coat. The orchard, with its neat rows of pear, apple and plum trees, was already looking ready for that night's fun. The wood for the bonfire was piled into an impressively large peak. Tony, with the help of several village boys, was using long sticks to check under the wood for any hedgehogs who might be unwittingly hiding under there. *Dear boy,* smiled Flora, *making sure no innocent little hedgehog gets burnt.*

Mr Adams and Nurse Smythson had already put up a few of the trestle tables and Flora placed the plate on the nearest one. As she turned to go back to the house, she nearly collided with Busby. He was carrying armfuls of colourful bunting.

At the sight of his broad shoulders and unruly rust-coloured hair, she felt her pulse quicken. They hadn't seen each other since their argument at the funeral. Flora had had enough time to reflect on her behaviour. *Perhaps I shouldn't have been so angry, or at least I should have been more diplomatic. After all Busby did have a job to do.*

She scanned his expression to try and assess how he was feeling about her. *Is he still flipping furious?* There was just enough of a smile around his lips and the hint of a twinkle about his amber eyes to encourage Flora to ask, 'Truce?'

His smile broadened as he confirmed, 'Truce.'

She relaxed and beamed up at him. There was a distracting flurry of activity around their ankles. Dorothy had obviously heard her beloved Busby's voice and had somehow managed to free herself. Totally besotted, she gazed up at Busby, frantically wagging her tail while her lead trailed behind her.

He laughed and bent down to pick her up. He was just about able to hold her, along with the bunting. After he had suitably petted and fussed over her, Flora was able to eagerly ask, 'Are you here looking for suspects?'

'Actually, Mrs Honour has put me on bonfire and bunting duty.' To demonstrate, he held up his arms which were overflowing with dachshund and bunting. He smiled broadly. 'Anyway, surely part of the truce is you not asking inappropriate questions? And I'm happy to pretend that I don't have a bone to pick with you.'

Dorothy began wriggling and yapping, the combination of being in Busby's arms and the mention of the magical word 'bone' was too much for her. Flora decided it was safer if she took charge of her hound. With a mild word of admonition, she placed Dorothy on the ground while firmly holding onto her lead.

'Are you coming tonight?' she asked, trying not to smile too brightly as she was aware the eyes of the village were upon her. 'As part of your village duties, of course, and in no way related to any investigations you may or nor be making.'

Busby appeared to hesitate.

'I will give you an extra slice of excellent apple pie,' she coaxed.

He raised an eyebrow. 'You cooked it?'

Horrified, Flora stammered, 'Of course not! But my Mrs Wilkes cooked it, so it's classified as my contribution.'

There was a hint of a smile playing around his mouth. 'How convenient for you.'

She held his gaze for a second before smiling, 'But I will be serving it – and wearing an apron – which is not a sight you will often see.'

'So, it's sort of your version of being Marie Antoinette?'

Flora raised her eyebrows. 'Sorry I don't see what my supply of apple pie for the village has to do with French royalty.' He was grinning now and Flora was aware a couple of village women were staring at them.

'She liked playing at being just like everyone else and wearing her wealth lightly,' he said.

Flora gave a mock frown. 'Is that a compliment or an insult?' She knew from the admiring looks he was giving her that insulting her was the last thing on his mind.

He stopped smiling and looked serious. 'Perhaps it's neither. Perhaps it's just me expressing my unease at the difference in our backgrounds.'

There was a faint concentration line between his eyes and Flora had the fleeting thought that she would rather like to kiss his worry line away.

*Goodness, this is getting interesting, but it is neither the time or the place for a deep and meaningful conversation about class, wealth, and the injustice of society – or for an impromptu kiss – not with half the village watching.*

As loathe as she was to leave Busby, her inner voice of wisdom was whispering, *you really should return to the sanctuary of the kitchen and away from all these watchful eyes.*

'I prefer to think of it as *noblesse oblige* – me doing my bit for the village.' Her smile broadened. 'Anyway, that quip would be more appropriate for you to make at the Lords and Ladies Ball.'

*Good Lord – help! I need rescuing while I still have a shred of my reputation left.*

# CHAPTER 5

## HOUSE GUESTS

Flora had never thought of her goddaughter as one of the Good Lord's ministering angels but the moment Lavinia wafted into the orchard, unsuitably dressed in furs and heels, she rendered Busby open-mouthed and speechless. Tony, as if drawn by a siren's call, suddenly appeared and stood by Busby with a similar expression of awe on his face.

Debo, hurrying past with a tray heaped with cups, gave out, 'What-oh, Lavinia! I'll just dump these,' she nodded at the cups, 'and be right back to say a proper hello.'

As she scurried off, Flora gave Lavinia a peck on the cheek. 'How lovely to see you dear. You are frightfully early; I wasn't expecting you till teatime. Still, it's no problem; there is plenty to do so your help will be welcome.'

Lavinia gave Flora a pitying look accompanied by a little tinkling laugh. 'Oh Flora, darling, I'm not so much early as most frightfully late.'

Flora looked baffled.

'Late for bed that is. Such a fun party last night, or was it parties? So hard to tell. Anyway there didn't seem much point in going home so I just came straight here.'

Debo returned and hugged Lavinia, while Flora surveyed the chaos of the kitchen and murmured, 'So we need to find you some breakfast.'

'Just a pot of coffee or tea at a pinch will suit me.'

A new thought struck Flora, she glanced around. 'No…' She wanted to say 'Lizard' but felt that wasn't his real name.

Lavinia frowned which only made her pert little face prettier. 'No, he's a frightful bore. I won't be seeing him again.'

'Gosh that was quick,' declared Debo, 'You seemed frightfully chummy a day or so ago when I came back from school.'

'He was such a child.' Lavinia sighed with the air of aged wisdom. 'What I need is an older man.'

Tony looked crestfallen and Flora didn't care for the way Lavinia was eyeing up Busby. Dorothy sensed the shift in Lavinia's interest and gave a low growl. *Paws off! He's mine!*

Lavinia continued to look wistfully at a blushing Busby as she huskily mused, 'I need someone who is mature and steady and who can whisk me off my feet.' She fluttered her eyelashes becomingly in Busby's direction.

Flora decided to take command of the conversation. *I am not about to have my goddaughter make any rash alliances under my roof, especially if it involves Busby.* Crisply she stated, 'I think you will find, dear, that mature men don't go in much for whisking anyone anywhere. When it comes to finding a life partner, I would advise you examine his bank account and look at how interfering his relations may be. Many a budding marriage has been ruined by lack of funds and a difficult mother-in-law.'

Lavinia blinked at Flora. 'Where's your romantic soul?' Thoughtfully and totally without malice merely stating a fact, she added, 'I assume it fades with age.'

'Well really!' muttered Flora, pressing her lips together.

Lavinia regarded Flora with wide, innocent eyes. 'You weren't always such a stick-in-the-mud. Your elopement with Uncle Roger is still the scandal of the county.'

Debo swung round to face Flora. 'Really, Mother?'

Flora flushed but Lavinia hadn't finished. 'You'd only known him for a day.'

Defensively Flora declared, 'Actually, it was a whole weekend – a rather jolly house party in Norfolk.' She carefully avoided meeting Busby's gaze and in business-like mode hurried Lavinia back to the house and up to her room.

Having settled one house guest, she returned downstairs to find her other invitee in the hallway.

Great Aunt Gigi filled any room from the moment she entered it, in much the same way that she had once dominated the London stage. She was Flora's favourite and most flamboyant aunt. As ever, she looked fabulous. Hair that should be grey with age was a shimmering gold, like a field of barley ready for harvest. The few wrinkles she did have were soft and her complexion was healthy. She had embraced fashionably short hair and hem lines with a youthful zeal.

Long before the turn of the previous century, Gigi had been a young exotic dancer on the London stage. To the family's horror, she had captured the heart of Flora's great uncle. Legend had it that after the first glimpse of her dainty ankle, artistically displayed with the aid of two large, pink ostrich feather fans, he had fallen madly in love with her.

So, she had ended up noted as a 'Lady' in Debrett's and one of the wealthiest women in the kingdom. As she liked to comment, with a laugh, 'Not bad for a girl who grew up in a children's home.'

She was not alone; with her were two of the most beautiful young men Flora had ever had the pleasure of laying her eyes on. Tall and blonde with dazzling blue eyes and chiselled features, they were the answer to a maiden's dream.

'Flora, darling!' enthused Great Aunt Gigi, enveloping her in a warm hug and a mist of perfume. 'Meet my beautiful boys.' She presented them with all the flare of a magician pulling a rabbit, or rather two, out of a hat. Identical twins, both were well over six foot tall and devastatingly good looking.

'Flora, may I present Pierre and Anton BeauFrere? I might add that they dance beautifully.'

The pair smiled affably at Flora as they shook her hand, and she knew she would never be able to tell them apart.

Her own little maiden, Debo, seemed less interested in the young men and more intent on quizzing Great Aunt Gigi. 'We have the gramophone in the library and I'm sure Mummy has some suitably jolly tunes, but I am not sure what we can use as an outsized pink flamingo feathered fan.'

'What fun!' declared Gigi. 'But first, my dear, let me just settle a bit of admin with your mother.' She turned her dazzling smile on Flora. 'I do hope it isn't a problem me bringing my boys with me.'

Flora happily affirmed, 'Not at all. I can put them in the twin room I had made up for Lavinia's Lizard.'

Great Aunt Gigi raised an eyebrow and murmured, 'How frightfully vivarium.'

It was at this moment that Mrs Honour marched into the hall with a couple of baskets in hand.

'Ah! Mrs Honour, let me introduce my aunt and her – er – her friends.'

Great Aunt Gigi scrutinized Mrs Honour, and her smile disappeared. 'We've met before.'

Curtly Mrs Honour snapped, 'I think not.' She ran a critical eye over Great Aunt Gigi. 'I am sure I would have remembered. Now if you'll excuse me, I have things to do.'

With that, she swept out. Flora watched her depart and when she was safely out of earshot remarked, 'She always makes me feel inadequate – as if I'm not pulling my weight.'

Great Aunt Gigi tucked a companionable arm in Flora's. 'That is her intention, my dear child. The best thing to do is ignore her, preferably while drinking champagne. Do you have any?'

'Any what?' asked Flora.

'Champagne.'

'At three o'clock in the afternoon?'

'No matter, I had my beautiful boys pack cases of the stuff.' She let an appreciative eye rest on the two fine young men, who smiled back her. 'They are heavenly, aren't they?'

'Positively angelic,' agreed Flora as they went to the car to fetch the much-needed champagne.

Nanny walked in and stopped at the sight of Aunt Gigi. The contrast between the two older ladies could not have been greater.

For her part, Aunt G regarded Nanny with a raised eyebrow and no sign of a smile. 'Nanny. Not dead yet?'

Nanny's small hedgehog eyes twinkled and when she spoke, she sounded rather more Irish than was her norm. 'What, and miss the chance to dance on your grave?'

Aunt Gigi laughed. '*Touché!*'

Nanny nodded towards the boys. 'New pets?'

'I find them so much more congenial than a paid companion. Why is it paid companions always look so limp – they seem to wilt before one's eyes. I would find having one constantly around would be most lowering to the spirits.'

Nanny grunted. 'Nothing wilted or limp about them.'

'Where's Lavinia? I want to have a serious talk to her about her future. Gossip has it that she is spending all her time chasing after one unsuitable boy after another. What that girl needs is a job.'

Debo said, 'What, on the stage, with feathers like yours?'

'No, dear, Lavinia has looks but no curves. I was thinking the movies.'

# CHAPTER 6

## *A RATHER EVENTFUL FIREWORKS PARTY*

'Have you shut Dorothy away?' asked Nanny.

Flora nodded as she struggled to get her gumboots on. 'Yes, she is safely tucked away in my room with the shutters closed and both a fire and a fresh bone to keep her company. I don't think the fireworks will bother her.'

'That's a mercy,' muttered Nanny. 'Now if you've got your boots on, let's walk down to the orchard together.'

The evening was cold, damp and dark. Flora could smell the bonfire long before she could see it.

'Quite a magnificent blaze!' she commented to Busby when she was close enough to be heard. He grinned back at her, evidently enjoying his role of chief bonfire stoker.

Tony and the two beautiful boys walked up with their arms ladened with logs.

'These are all dry – I took them from the pile we keep for the house,' beamed Tony proudly.

*My dry logs? Why not the wood from the stables? Oh well, I guess I'll just have to resign myself to a Christmas with dismal fires and damp logs.*

Trestle tables, brimming over with food stood close by, watched over by a few village matrons. Nanny had taken command of the tea urn. Flora's young maids, Gladys and Mavis, were giggling and handing out the cups. Over-excited children were running and screaming all over the orchard while their weary mothers weakly warned, 'Mind the bonfire.'

Flora was surprised to see Paul there; those who had had a bad time of it in the trenches tended to avoid fireworks. *Presumably, the dear man didn't want to disappoint his daughter.* He was pushing a wide-eyed Betty in a wheelbarrow, with pillows around her and a blanket over her legs. The child was over excited; she fidgeted in the makeshift carriage and her chatter was high pitched and fast. Claire was rosy cheeked and beaming.

Flora smiled at them. 'Good evening.' Claire and Betty warmly greeted her back. Paul merely grunted.

Nurse Smythson arrived, dressed in sensible boots and a thick wool coat that had seen better days but was obviously good quality. 'What can I do to help, Mrs Farrington?'

Flora thought this was rather brave as the last time she'd asked that question she got landed with a load of trestle tables.

'Goodness only knows, but if you ask Nanny, over there by the tea urn, I'm sure she'll come up with loads of useful things for you to do.'

'Wait for me, Nurse Smythson. I'd like to lend a hand too,' called Derek Adams as he hurried up.

Flora glanced at him. *At least he is looking a little brighter than when I last saw him, but goodness, where did he get that overcoat and suit? I didn't know it was possible to buy such shockingly bright tweed.* Instead of commenting on his tasteless tweed she simply said, 'How kind, and how brave of you to come.'

His smile didn't quite reach his sorrowful eyes. It suggested courage rather than happiness. 'To be honest, the house is so empty without Maud and I fear I would only mope if I spent the evening sitting there all alone.'

The pair went to talk to Nanny.

Above the gentle crackle of the bonfire, Flora heard a high-pitched whine. 'My shoes will be ruined! What a ridiculous place to hold a fireworks display.'

Flora looked over to where Dr Honour, his mother and a beautiful young woman were picking their way, torch in hand. Flora regarded the speaker: *Lady Clarke I presume.*

Dr Honour, with ill-disguised impatience snapped, 'An orchard is an eminently suitable place for fireworks. Perhaps you should have chosen different shoes.'

Lady Clarke was totally unabashed by the doctor's rebuke. She gave a tinkling laugh and murmured, 'Oh Victor, you are a tease.'

Dr Honour grunted through pursed lips, 'I should go and help Busby and Tony with setting up the fireworks.'

'Nonsense!' declared Mrs Honour briskly. 'You need to take Lady Clarke's arm; you don't want her to stumble.' Flora noted that Dr Honour's expression suggested he really didn't care a jot if she stumbled or not.

Mrs Honour was scanning the trestle tables, where the food was invitingly piled on platters and apron-clad ladies were handing out steaming cups of mulled wine and mini sausages on sticks. 'I, on the other hand, am definitely needed over there, if all the food is not to be handed out before even the first firework has gone off.'

She strode purposefully away. With her gone, Flora considered it safe to go up to the little party of lady Clarke and Dr Honour. As she walked across the orchard, Lavinia wandered up to her. Flora greeted her, privately thinking, *Thank goodness she has changed from furs and high heels to boots and tweeds.*

'This is rather jolly, isn't it?' exclaimed Lavinia, suddenly reminding Flora of the enthusiastic schoolgirl she had been, before she morphed into a sophisticated socialite.

To Flora's surprise Lavinia stiffened when her eyes alighted on Lady Clarke. Flora acknowledged the doctor and Lady Clarke. She was about to introduce Lavinia when her goddaughter said without any trace of warmth, 'We know each other from Town.'

(Town meaning London as, for the young set, London was the only town worth mentioning.)

Lady Clarke regarded Lavinia through narrow eyes and curled her lip before saying, 'Only vaguely as we hardly mix in the same circles.'

Flora chose to ignore the evident hostility between the two gorgeous girls, and said brightly, 'Oh and here are Mr Adams and Nurse Smythson, both hard at work.'

They were both carrying trays of mince pies. Flora could

not help noticing that Nurse Smythson was wearing impeccably suitable boots. Flora thought she detected a fleeting look of approval and admiration from Dr Honour but doubted that it was just for her choice in footwear. Nurse Smythson for her part, looked straight through Dr Honour, as if he did not exist. Derek jovially offered them all mince pies before murmuring that they needed to circulate before the pies got cold.

As they walked away Lavinia commented, 'He's awfully brave, handing out mince pies when he has just lost his wife.'

Flora was just thinking of a suitable response when Debo ran up. Her eyes were sparkling and voice full of excitement.' Oh Mummy, it's too thrilling, the fireworks are about to start.'

'Wonderful dear, I was about to suggest to Lavinia and Lady Clarke that we watch them from over there by the hedge. We should have a good view there, and the ground isn't too wet.'

'Right oh, I'm going to watch it from by the bonfire,' declared Debo as she ran off.

Lavinia and Lady Clarke were still eyeing each other up in much the same way as two boxers assess their opponent before a knockout fight, leading Flora to think, *I had better distract them before the first punch is thrown.*

'Well, ladies,' she smiled at Dr Honour, 'and gentleman, shall we move over to that spot by the hedge? I think Lady Clarke, you will find it quite dry there. We need to hurry as we don't want to miss any of the fireworks.'

'If we must,' said Lady Clarke with all the enthusiasm of a dead fish. 'Although when one has seen the fireworks at Monte Carlo, all other fireworks seem nothing more than a damp squib. Victor, give me your arm – the ground is too infernally uneven here.'

While internally bristling – *damp squib indeed!* – Flora managed to be a gracious host and lead the way.

They reached the spot just as the first firework exploded high in the air. The flowering of red sparks in the sky was swiftly accompanied by a deafening bang. Unexpectedly two small boys crashed into their party. They were so intent on their game of chase that even fireworks didn't deter them. Lady Clarke would have been knocked off her feet had she not got a claw-like hand on Dr Honour's strong arm. Even so, the incident drew a very unladylike expletive from Lady Clarke's lips, leading Flora to think, *she really is a pill of the first order. I am rapidly joining Lavinia in my antipathy towards Dr Honour's intended.*

In amongst all the chaos, the bangs and brilliant fireworks only added to the confusion.

Once all were righted and the boys had run off, Flora jovially commented, 'Gosh that last one sounded as if it was rather too close for comfort. My ears are ringing.'

Dr Honour and Lavinia made muffled sounds of agreement, but they were only half listening as they joined the rest of the village in craning their necks towards the heavens and uttering loud 'Oohs' and 'Ahs' as bursts of colour unfolded in the dark skies above them. Flora was satisfied to note that even Lady Clarke had lost some of her Monte Carlo scorn and uttered a few sighs of appreciation.

Wafts of the woman's rather too overpowering perfume assailed Flora. *Goodness, if it's this strong out in the open, what on earth would it be like if one was sharing a sofa with the lady, let alone a tight embrace? No wonder Dr Honour is keen to avoid getting embroiled with her.* With a mental shudder she concluded, *One can't help imagining that marriage to her would involve a lifetime of asphyxiation by overpriced but fashionable scent.*

She shuffled her feet in order to put more space between them. As she edged closer to the hedge her toe touched something. It had a vaguely squidgy feel. Curiously, Flora glanced down, flashing her torch at the ground.

She blinked, not quite believing her eyes. She focused her light on the obstacle and tried to make sense of what she was looking at. As her mind confirmed what her eyes were seeing, her body froze. She fumbled with the torch and stumbled backwards. Lavinia and Lady Clarke both stopped staring at the sky and stared at her.

Flora pointed a shaky finger at the ground unable to speak.

Lavinia trained her torch to where Flora was pointing.

Sticking out from the hedge, was a man's leg, clad in a garish tweed which could only belong to Derek Adams. The rest of his body was hidden under the foliage, but this limb lay unnaturally still in the damp evening air.

Lavinia's screams rose above the sounds of the crackling bonfire, the cries of the over-excited children and even the last pops of the fireworks.

With her heart pounding and her mind racing, Flora sensed someone standing close by. She waved her torch's beam; by its light she could clearly see Paul standing immobile, his face blank, his eyes staring into nothing. In his hand was a pistol, a German Luger, a common souvenir from the trenches.

The only person who did not scream was Dr Honour. Ignoring Paul, he was straight down on his knees by Derek's unmoving body. '*Light*!' he shouted. 'I need light.' Flora had just enough of her senses intact to shine her torch's beam in the general direction, but her hands were shaking so badly that it was not that helpful.

Nurse Smythson appeared and in a brisk no-nonsense sort of a way she took Flora's torch. With calm control she used both her own and Flora's torch beams to shine over Derek as the doctor examined him. Her heart still pounding, Flora regarded the body. *Lucky we have an abundance of medics to deal.*

Lavinia stopped screaming and lent the light of her torch, too. Lady Clarke was threatening to swoon but seeing that no one was paying her any attention, she changed her mind.

Flora turned her attention to Paul. He looked glazed. Eventually, he focused glassy eyes upon her and said, 'I didn't do it.'

'But why are you holding that pistol?' asked Flora with more curiosity than sense.

He glanced down at it, blinked in surprise then looked back to Flora, his mouth hanging open.

Slightly late but nonetheless in dashing mode, Busby and the beautiful boys arrived at a run. Efficient and in command Busby grabbed Paul's wrist with both hands.

'Drop it!' he commanded in a voice that expected instant compliance. Paul made no resistance, he didn't even attempt to flee. Meekly he allowed Busby to take the gun.

The beautiful boys were either side of him and he collapsed between them and would have sunk to the ground had they not held him up.

An animal-like howl erupted from Claire. Her normally happy face was contorted with anguish. She was trembling and wide eyed with terror. Betty started to howl with confusion. Flora was pleased when two of the village ladies took a hand and bustled the distraught pair away.

Flora glanced back at Derek Adams.

'He's going to be fine,' said Dr Honour, as he stood up. Flora could not help noticing that the knees of his trousers were wet from the damp grass, or perhaps from Mr Adams' blood.

The curious crowd of onlookers gave at a collective sigh. Flora wasn't sure if it was from relief or disappointment.

'But why is there so much blood?' queried Flora, fighting back a wave of nausea at the sight.

'His ear was cut. Ears always do bleed,' stated Nurse Smythson. Derek Adams stirred. 'Just lie still,' she commanded in a voice that demanded obedience.

'So, the bullet missed and just grazed his ear?' persisted Flora.

Dr Honour shook his head. 'The bullet did miss, but the cut was caused by something else. He must have caught it on something sharp when he fainted.'

Busby nodded and started to lead a unresisting Paul Draycott away. 'Stand back!' he commanded as curious villagers pressed around them. Busby held his prisoner firmly. He clenched his jaw and marched while Draycott's expression was blank and his steps dragged.

Instinctively, Flora put herself in front of Busby and Paul Draycott, declaring, 'You can't do this.'

Busby's hazel eyes flashed angrily at Flora and through tight lips he hissed, 'Mrs Farrington, you need to stay out of this and mind your own business.'

Busby and Flora were so focused on each other that they didn't care that over half the village was listening and watching them with open-mouthed fascination.

Thrusting her chin up, fists clenched by her sides, she would have liked to have spoken with cold dignity but she could feel the tears burning behind her eyes and threatening to spill down her cheeks. Her voice came out as angry, hurried and high pitched. 'This is my business.'

His eyes were sharp and his voice hard as he spat back, 'Why?' His eyes bore into her. She started to stammer something, but he hadn't finished. 'Because you are the lady of the manor and you have a duty of noblesse oblige to the villagers?' He sounded sad and exasperated. 'For goodness's sake, Flora, the world doesn't operate like that, not since the war destroyed a whole generation of young men.'

'But what about Claire? What about the child? What will become of them? Have you thought about them?' Her cry was part wail and part shout.

His nostrils flared and she could see a vein throbbing on his temple. 'Of course I've thought about them, but my job is to arrest murderers and protect innocents.'

Flora threw her hands in the air. Her voice trembling with rage, she said in a voice she tried to keep low, 'But Claire and Betty are innocents. I don't think you realise what sort of a life you are committing them to if you arrest Paul and have him hung.'

Busby glowered down at her. Their eyes had been locked throughout their exchange but now his amber eyes took on an added fire. His every muscle was taut with anger, he was breathing heavily, and his voice became dangerously quiet. 'No Flora, it's you who have no idea what sort of life Paul Draycott's family are in for. You sit in your ivory tower of wealth and privilege, totally protected from the harsh realities of life.'

Stung, she stared at him, then quietly she said, 'How dare you say that to me?' She blinked hard, trying not to cry, but despite all her efforts a single tear escaped and ran down her cheek. 'Need I remind you that I am a widow? I know what it's like to lose the person you love and to face raising children all alone.'

As he replied his voice was slightly softer but still firm. 'You have always been protected by having money. You never had to worry about your children starving.'

Flora stood, winded by his words. She took a slow steadying breath and regarded him with a glacial gaze. Drawing herself to her full height, she looked him in the eye and with cold, firm, dignity said, 'Inspector Busby, you are in the wrong. Mr Draycott is innocent, and I shall prove it.'

# CHAPTER 7

## AUNT GIGI

The next day Flora still had an emotional hangover from the fight with Busby and the tragic events with the Draycott family. Her own family suffered no such sensibility.

She heard the jolly music coming from the library long before she reached the door. Happy notes reverberated throughout the house. *Goodness, Gigi must have the gramophone playing at full blast.*

When Flora opened the library door she was greeted by a lively scene, Debo was being expertly whirled around the room by Anton – or was it Pierre? His long limbs and blonde locks were in sharp contrast to Debo's childish height and wild brown curls, but they were both evidently having fun. Meanwhile, Aunt Gigi, a vision in pink silk, was dancing with the other beautiful boy. Nanny sat on the sofa, stoically knitting, dressed in her habitual black. She was doing a good impression of not noticing the mayhem all around. Lavinia was lazily flicking through a periodical. The fire was blazing and a pot of tea sat on the side, as well the most lavish box of chocolates that Flora had seen for a while. She popped one in her mouth and sat down next to Lavinia to enjoy the spectacle of the dancers. *Is that the foxtrot or the shimmy?*

As Gigi twirled close to Lavinia, she announced, 'Lavinia darling, with your looks you could be in films.'

Lavinia wrinkled her pert little nose, fluttered her long eyelashes and replied, 'Not all of us want to prostitute our looks for money.' She was wearing a sapphire-blue day dress which was more demure than her normal attire and set off her eyes magnificently.

Gigi laughed. 'What do you propose to do with your life?'

Lavinia sat up straight in her chair and declared, 'Matrimony is a woman's highest calling.'

Flora nearly choked on her chocolate. *Matrimony? Highest calling? Where is the party girl who arrived in a short dress and accompanied by a lizard only a day or two ago?*

Gigi was being expertly dipped by her partner but when she was the right way up, she laughing said, 'And looks are not involved in snagging a husband? Now, matrimony really could be termed as prostitution.' She was twirled around and forced to be silent for a second before she was able to call over to Flora's happy dancing daughter, 'Debo, do you understand the word *prostitution*?'

Debo, mid-pirouette, grinned. 'Oh rather! Oldest profession and all that. It tends to crop up in scripture lessons – Sodom and Gomorrah, don't you know.'

Gigi smiled contentedly. 'Excellent, I do believe in girls having a solid education in theology.'

Both Gigi, Debo and the beautiful boys danced some more before Gigi paused to catch her breath and again addressed Lavinia. 'And what do you propose to do before you embark on your highest calling? Knit?' Here she glanced at the industrious Nanny who ignored both her and her comment.

'Good works!' declared Lavinia with surprising determination as she rose to her feet. 'Speaking of which, I might go and visit Mr Adams. He is so brave.'

'I really wouldn't, if I were you,' replied Gigi.

'Well, you are not me!' declared Lavinia as she flounced from the room.

Flora sighed. 'Oh dear, Lavinia seems to be entering a worthy phase. Is that more or less worrying than her being reckless and carefree?'

'I wouldn't know, dear,' said Gigi. 'I pride myself on never having had a worthy phase.' She stopped dancing and addressed her partner. 'Be a dear and follow the child. Discreetly, mind. We don't want her getting into any trouble.'

He nodded and left while Flora wished once again that she could tell the twins apart.

'Speaking of good works, Nanny,' said Flora, picking up Lavinia's discarded periodical and glancing at it, 'I thought I might take a basket of goodies to the Draycott home. You know the sort of thing, eggs, fruitcake and whatnots.'

'Good idea, you can take this for Betty, I have nearly finished it.' Nanny held up a beautiful little cardigan.

Gigi graciously sat down on the sofa next to them and helped herself to a glass of water from the crystal jug on a tray. She sipped it. The dancing had brought a becoming pink glow to her cheeks. Her healthy complexion was complemented by the blush tones in her dress.

As the song wound to a close, Debo and her partner decided that they would also prefer to sit for a moment. They both seemed uninterested in making use of either armchair or sofas and comfortably curled up on the floor in front of the fire. Debo set up the chess set and undoubtably they would have enjoyed a fine game had Dorothy not decided to join them and knock over all the pieces.

'Really Dorothy?' exclaimed Debo mildly, before adding, 'I am going to have a slice of cake, would you like some, Anton?'

He agreed enthusiastically and set about restraining Dorothy.

Gigi was gazing wistfully into the fire's dancing flames when she commented with a sigh, 'The people I have met who are the most determined to be do-gooders are usually trying to compensate for being pretty stinking personalities.'

From beneath her haphazardly-pinned mops of silver curls, Nanny glanced up. She nodded in agreement, and above the rhythmic clicking of her knitting needles added, 'Life is full of those sorts of things.'

'What sort of things?' asked Debo through a mouthful of fruit cake.

'Things that look one way but are rather another,' explained Nanny.

'Oh,' said Debo, 'I thought you were about to say something

along the lines of, how unjust it is that good people die while evil folk prosper.'

Gigi frowned. 'I'm glad you've realised that – it's as well to come to terms with the injustice of life while you are young. It will make the rest of your life far more enjoyable.' Her sombre moment soon gave way to her habitual gaiety, as she smiled brightly. 'Of course there are times when justice is done – like Maud Adams drowning.'

Flora's eyes widened and her mouth fell open in surprise. She stared at Gigi while everyone else appeared unaffected by her words. Nanny continued knitting, Debo and Anton were trying to set up the chessboard once more with Dorothy's help.

'You knew Maud?' was all Flora could think to ask.

'Not directly, but I was aware of the woman as a collector of other people's secrets. She was an unpleasant soul who liked to use the information she had gleaned to toy with the emotions of her victims.'

Flora agreed. 'She was always like that. When we were at school, she found out that Gertie was stuffing socks in her brassiere to make herself look more – well, you know. She made poor Gertie's life a misery, threatening to tell everyone.'

Debo looked up. 'What happened?'

'Well, I found out and informed poor Gertie that we were all doing it and instantly Maud's threats lost all their power.'

As she continued her knitting, Nanny flashed Gigi a shrewd look, her small black eyes shining. 'I suspect that your knowledge of Maud was rather more serious than socks in a brassiere?'

Gigi nodded. 'I had a dear young friend who I was very fond of and she suffered terribly because of Maud's delight in playing cat and mouse with other people's lives. She seemed to take pleasure in playing with her victims' deepest fears for her own amusement.'

'So what was your friend's weakness that Maud uncovered?' enquired Flora, finding Gigi's story far more interesting than the periodical she had been glancing at.

'A baby,' said Gigi simply. 'To my mind the arrival of a baby should always be celebrated, regardless of whether it comes within wedlock or out.'

Debo looked up from the chessboard. 'That's what Mummy always says. Isn't that so?'

She looked at Flora, who nodded and added, 'Going back to your comment about justice and Maud: are you saying that you feel that whoever bumped her off did the world a service?'

There was a slight crease between Flora's brows as she came grips with the fact that a beloved relative might believe a spot of murder was quite acceptable given the right circumstances.

Gigi thoughtfully swirled her drink. 'Not quite. But I do believe the world is a better place because she is not in it.'

'Same thing,' stated Debo, moving her bishop.

Gigi replied easily, 'No, it isn't. The first suggests I condone murder.'

Relieved that Gigi did actually possess a recognisable moral compass, Flora nodded. 'Quite. After all, murder is always wrong.'

Gigi grinned. 'Not necessarily.'

Flora decided it was time to change the subject. 'If Lavinia is so keen to make Derek Adams the recipient of her benevolence, I wonder if I shouldn't invite the man over here, to save her from going there and throwing herself at him? Also, we would be able to nip in the bud any tendencies she might have for being desperately over-earnest. After all, we are quite a jolly crew.'

Gigi rolled her eyes. 'I have spent a lifetime avoiding tragic widowers and I will not have you inflict one on me now.'

Flora sighed. 'I can't understand why she wants to spend time with an old chap like Derek Adams rather than a bright young thing like Lady Clarke. I would have thought they would have become the best of chums by now – lots in common and all that – but they seem to loathe each other.

There was a silence. Flora was aware that Gigi, Nanny and Debo were all exchanging meaningful, if slightly amused, looks. Only Dorothy and Anton were not participating, both being more interested in the chess pieces.

'What?' she asked, a touch defensively.

Debo enlightened her. 'Oh Mummy, they are both extremely young and beautiful. Before Lavinia came over all pious, they both loved the London life.'

'Exactly, they have a lot of shared interests. By rights they should be the best of friends.'

Debo sighed. 'Sometimes I do wonder how you could have lived so long and learnt so little.'

Flora thought she detected slight nods of agreement from Gigi and Nanny.

'You've lost me,' she confessed.

'They both like to be the centre of attention, the Queen Bee. Far from seeing each other as comrades, they regard each other as competition.'

# CHAPTER 8

## *FLORA AND CLAIRE FACE HARSH REALITY*

Claire's home might be warm and tranquil, but her mind was in turmoil. The kitchen range was burning, the coppers gleamed, her child was serenely sleeping on her knee as she rocked gently to and fro while her mind raced in an endless hopeless spiral.

*He'd been so different before the war. If only the war had never happened; if only we had never met Maud Adams; if only I hadn't cajoled Paul into going to the fireworks.*

She took a deep calming breath. *I mustn't give way – I can't. What would happen to Betty?*

Claire looked down at the sleeping child in her arms. Her blonde curls, her round cheeks and her steady breath were all perfect. *I really should put another log in the range, but I don't want to move – she's bound to wake and she looks so peaceful.* Tears prickled her eyes, threatening to fall.

Her head pounded with the same hopeless thoughts swirling hopelessly round and round in her mind. *What's to become of the babe? How can I keep her safe when she may well grow up without a dad? People will point at her and whisper. How will we live with the shame? We'll be forever linked to Draycott the murderer.*

At this point, Claire rocked some more in her rocking chair. It was about the only thing she had from her mother. It was comforting to think that she had been rocked in just the same way nearly a quarter of a century before. She glanced around the kitchen, trying to distract the thoughts from the reality of her life. Suddenly the paper chains that had looked so festive the day before jarred. The tears began to flow, silent hopeless tears.

*How will I be able to earn enough money to stop us from starving? Where will we live? This cottage belongs to Mr Adams and goes with the job – he will need it for his next gardener.* A new wave of tears coursed down her face as the spectre of the workhouse swam before her eyes.

*How could we have come to this? Before the war, Paul had been renowned as the gentlest boy in the village.* Once, she had seen him release a baby rabbit from a snare because he couldn't bear to kill it. *How had he managed in the trenches when he was expected to kill far more than rabbits?*

She shuddered as her mind switched to the other night. *How in the world did he go from the gentle soul he was then, to the man he is now? I wonder* – she swallowed, *I wonder, did he do it? Have I been sharing a bed with a murderer? Lately it's been a relief when he'd get up in the early hours and began his nightly prowling.*

With an effort, she took her thoughts to the early days of their relationship. As a child she'd followed him around like a little stray puppy. She smiled as she remembered how he was always good natured about it, however much the other village boys teased him.

She'd been heartbroken when she, along with the rest of the village, had waved him off to war. When he came back on leave, she'd already made her mind up that he wouldn't go back to the front without their relationship having graduated from girlish infatuation to adult 'intended'. The first time he'd kissed her – or rather she'd kissed him – he'd been so shy about it. He was by nature timid despite his bulk.

The ensuing months had been hell; she'd been so fearful every time she saw the telegraph boy. When he was invalided out of the war she had been filled with joy. Now her stomach clenched. *I didn't know then that a man can be physically safe but have his mind always on the battlefield.*

It was at this unfortunate moment that Flora bustled in, full of life and bonhomie. Inevitably this woke Betty, who blinked sleepy eyes at the intruder. Flora stood in the doorway and proffered the basket with a smile.

Suddenly, Claire found a focus for all her confusion and anger. Her own pride was about all that was holding her together. Her normally placid face contorted with rage. Glowering at Flora she spat, 'Mrs Farrington, you can just take your basket of unwanted trinkets and go. Betty and I don't need your charity.'

Flora was so surprised and hurt by Claire's unexpected outburst that she didn't know what to say. Silently, with her basket in hand, she turned to go, only to see Busby in the doorway. She didn't know how much he had overheard but guessed it would have been enough for him to gauge the situation.

Without making eye contact with him or saying a word, she brushed past him. Once outside she took big gulps of cold air, trying to regain her equilibrium. Her head swam and her knees threatened to buckle beneath her. The garden bench seemed her only option and much as she wanted to make a quick escape she had to sit for a moment.

She put the basket down beside her and with her thoughts in a turmoil she buried her face in her hands. Seconds later she felt a large handkerchief placed in her fingers and she realised she was crying and that Busby was beside her.

She took the hankie and between sobs said, 'If you have come to gloat, I really haven't got the strength to deal with it.'

His voice was deep and kind. 'She's overwrought, Flora. She didn't mean what she said.' He paused, swallowed and then said quietly, 'Just like I didn't mean what I said to you the other day.'

Flora sniffed and looked up at him with red-rimmed eyes. 'Yes she did, just as you meant every word you said when you arrested Paul.' She dabbed at her eyes with his handkerchief.

'About that, Flora, the other night, I feel perhaps I was too—' He was interrupted by her loudly blowing her nose on the same handkerchief.

'Thank you for this,' she murmured as she tried to hand it back to him back.

'That's quite alright, you keep it,' murmured Busby hastily. 'Look, I need to speak to Mrs Draycott, that's why I am here, so

I'll give her the basket. I am sure that now she has had time to calm down she'll be grateful.'

Flora nodded, sniffed again and walked away with drooping shoulders.

# CHAPTER 9

### DEBO IN DANGER

'Hey Tony, I have a smashing idea,' declared Debo as she half ran, half skipped into the garage, where Tony was 'fixing' Flora's Morgan.

'Hand me that spanner,' came a muffled voice from under the car's hood. He held out an oily hand and Debo dutifully passed him the nearest spanner. He paused for a second and then, exasperated, he rejected it. 'Not that one, idiot.' He reached for a different one.

The garage was originally a lofty barn that Roger and Flora had deemed should be used for cars rather than corn, so now the large Silver Ghost Rolls Royce and Flora's small red Morgan stood side by side. Even with the two vehicles, there was still acres of room with a work bench equipped with all the tools to keep them both in tip top condition.

It was cold in the garage and both of them were wrapped up in layers of woollies. *Tony's fingerless mittens will never be fit to wear again,* Debo thought. *Good thing Nanny is a whizz at knitting.*

Aloud she said, 'So my idea is, why don't you and I pop over to Derek Adams' house and do a spot of breaking and entering?' Her voice brimmed over with enthusiasm. Had Tony bothered to look up, he would have seen that her eyes were sparkling.

'Why on earth would we want to do that?' He didn't sound that interested.

'Why? To look for clues, of course,' exclaimed Debo, stamping her feet to keep the cold at bay and making her curls bounce.

Tony glanced over at her. 'What?'

Energised by having his attention she enthused, 'Clues as to who murdered Maud. It will be the most wonderful Christmas gift for Mummy. You know how worried and upset she is about Paul Draycott.'

Tony returned to his tinkering. 'The police will have already searched the place.'

'Really, Tony, have you never read a detective story? The police *always* miss the most important clues.'

To Debo's fury, Tony chuckled. 'You need to change your reading matter.'

'Well, what about trying just for Mummy?' Debo's was annoyed at herself as she heard the slight whine in her own voice. She was trying not to admit to herself that she was a little afraid of going to Derek's home alone.

Tony's comment was offhand. 'I'm sure Mother would far rather you gave her a book or a box of chocolates than you got yourself arrested for illegally breaking into Mr Adams' house. Now leave me alone; I'm busy.'

Debo stomped off; had she been able to slam the garage door she would have done so. *Well really! He's going to be pretty jealous when I'm the one who finds a vital clue and solves the case.*

She wandered into the house and before she had time to take off her coat, Flora walked past with her hands full of Christmas cards. She had a distinctly distracted air and her hair was ruffled. Dorothy trotted at her heels.

'Mother,' began Debo.

Flora barely glanced at her. 'Not now dear, I really am far too busy. I should at least try and write one or two Christmas cards. Of course, they won't arrive until the New Year. Why is it always the same every year? I always have every intention of getting them all done in November then the end of December rolls around and…' She shrugged as she disappeared into her study, and the last thing Debo heard before she shut the door was, 'And here we are *yet* again.'

No sooner had Flora left, Nanny bustled in with her red

carpetbag in hand and a determined look in her beetle-black eyes.

Debo smiled. *She's bound to be a willing ally.* 'Nanny?'

Nanny barely glanced her way as she muttered, 'Whatever it is, dear, it will just have to wait until after Christmas or better still the New Year.'

Debo watched her retreating back. She sighed and let her shoulders slump before she trudged with slow heavy steps out of the front door. The cold air hit her; it was bracing. She took a deep breath and lifted her head. 'I'll show them!' she declared out loud as she marched off to find her bicycle.

The ride to Derek Adams' house was invigorating. Debo arrived with her cheeks glowing and feeling quite warm with the exertion. She lost no time in hiding her bicycle behind a handy holly bush. It was covered in festive red berries. She smiled to herself. *Mummy is always lamenting that all the berries are gone by Christmas; she'd be very impressed by this bush.*

It was only now that she realised she hadn't quite thought things through. *How am I going to get into the house without anyone seeing me? And what can I say if someone finds me?* For the briefest of moments she wavered. *Perhaps I should just go home.* She tugged her coat straight and adjusted her beret. The memory of Tony's dismissive words came back to her. Turning her attention back to the task in hand, she swallowed and squared her shoulders.

*Here I go. I just need to slip in the back door unseen have a quick look round and find some vital clue implicating someone other than Mr Draycott in the murder of Mrs Adams. There are bound to be heaps of them: a blackmail letter or a threatening signed note or even a confession.*

She began to creep stealthily towards the house. She was extremely aware of every small sound she made. She was soon imagining herself as the intrepid American Indian she had seen recently, in all his flickering black-and-white glory, at the picture house. Like him, she took each step with care and skilfully avoided even snapping a twig underfoot.

When she was a few yards from the house, she had a moment of self-doubt. *Gosh the house looks rather big. I mean, it's not vast in the sense of stately home grandeur, actually it's quite modest in comparison to Farrington Hall but it's rather large with regard to square footage to search for a clue and still be home in time for lunch.*

She paused, looked at the dwelling again and, with determination, thought, *But if I don't at least try, I definitely won't be able to impress everyone.*

She was soon at the building and able to flatten herself against the walls. Mentally she switched characters and became the hero of the gangster film she had seen a while back. Like the film's hero she edged by the window and slowly lifted her head. *Of course, in the film, the chap was trying to avoid being spotted by the desperate gang of crooks who had kidnapped his lady love, whereas I'm just trying to avoid Mr Adams.*

The first window revealed the empty hallway and the second revealed Derek Adams and Nurse Smythson reading by the fire. *So that's them sorted; now where is Mrs Scrubs?*

It didn't take Debo long to locate her, in a side room, vigorously cleaning the silver. Her first thought was, *So the coast is clear for me to slip in the back door,* but before she could turn away, a large ginger tom cat jumped nimbly from the floor to the table and then up onto Mrs Scrubs' shoulder. Nuzzling lovingly against the housekeeper, the cat dislodged whatever hairpins had been holding up the woman's hair. As Debo watched in rapt amazement, a cascade of locks fell down the Mrs Scrubs' back. *Golly – I wouldn't have put that wizened stick down as having such a magnificent mane! Hints of ginger and curls to boot!* More surprises were to come. Far from being angry, Mrs Scrubs laughed and petted the cat. *My! Mummy is never going to believe this! Mrs Scrubs is awfully pretty when she smiles.* And if all these revelations were not enough, Mrs Scrubs then topped it all by starting to sing a folk song while affectionately caressing the feline. *Wonders will never cease! Even through the windowpane it's clear that Mrs Scrubs has a fine singing voice.*

It was with some reluctance that she pulled herself away from watching the surprising change in Mrs Scrubs. However, there were more shocks to come. As she was creeping towards the back of the house, Debo spotted Mrs Honour. Erect, stiff and sour-faced, she assumed the lady had come to call. For a second she was deflated. *Oh that's not going to help – Mrs Honour will be yet another person I need to avoid.* She watched the lady striding towards the house and experienced a wave of relief. *Actually, her arrival will probably work in my favour. She always likes to hold forth and lecture people, which will leave everyone trapped in one room for hours on end, leaving me free to carry out a detailed search.*

Leaving Mrs Honour to her own devices, Debo swiftly reached the back door. With a delicious mixture of fear and excitement, she entered.

The kitchen was warm with the range burning away. Debo paused to wonder, *Why doesn't Mrs Scrubs clean the silver in here where it's warm? Perhaps she doesn't want to make a mess.* She glanced at the kitchen table with interest. *But if that table has already been used as an operating table to take out Mrs Adams' appendix, surely a bit of silver polish wouldn't harm.*

With no particular answer coming to mind she decided to explore the rest of the house. She began to creep along the passageway which led from the kitchen to the main house. All her senses were heightened, she was alert for any sounds of approaching danger but at the same time, her confidence grew with every step she took.

Reaching the hall, she paused. The room was square and singularly unwelcoming to any would-be visitor: no weathered walking sticks and umbrellas in a brass stand, no carelessly tossed gloves on one side or piles of cards and letters from much-loved friends and family.

Debo glanced around. *Where should I start? I wonder if there is a study? Mummy always likes to say that she must pay some bills and check her accounts before going to her study and taking out her latest book and a box of chocolates.* Mrs Adams was *bound to have had a desk – I bet it's jam packed with clues. The only question is where?*

Debo was just looking around when she heard a movement behind her. She froze, a tingling running up her spine. She strained to hear more. *Who can that be?* She glanced over to the sitting-room door. *Nurse Smythson and Mr Adams are in there and Mrs Scrubs is over there.* She added as she took a quick look at the side door off the passageway behind her. With growing apprehension, she realised that whoever it was was coming closer.

*Where can I hide?*

In an instant she decided upon the cupboard under the stairs. Fortunately, the door opened without any creaking. Inside, it was a lot tidier than any of the cupboards at Farrington Hall. There was a neat new golf bag and that was about it.

Curiosity outweighed fear. *Who can it be?* she wondered as she carefully left the door open a crack.

She had only just secured herself within the cupboard and pressed her eye to the opening when the person crept into the hall with even more caution than Debo had deployed.

Debo blinked and stared in baffled incredulity. *Gosh, Mrs Honour? But why isn't she marching boldly into the sitting room to greet Mr Adams?*

As Debo watched, Mrs Honour looked around the hallway in much the same way that Debo had moments before.

More amazement was to come; Nurse Smythson's voice came clearly from just behind the closed sitting-room door. 'No, it's no trouble at all, Mr Adams, I am certain I saw the rug in the chest of drawers in the hallway.'

As the door handle turned, Debo saw Mrs Honour pale and hurriedly look around. *Goodness, she looks positively flustered. I always thought the old stick only had ice in her veins.*

Mrs Honour fixed her eyes on a far door and sped across the hall. As she opened it, Debo had a chance to glimpse the room beyond. *Ah! So that's where the study is.*

As Mrs Honour silently shut her door, Nurse Smythson swept into the hall. She walked straight to the chest of drawers, opened the bottom drawer and took out a folded, red rug. Rug in hand, she returned to the sitting room with a cheery, 'Here it is" and firmly shut the sitting room door.

Debo fixed her gaze on the study door while pondering, *I wonder if Mrs Honour will stay put for a bit longer? At least I now know where the study is – not that it's of much use with Mrs Honour in there.* She furrowed her brow. *And while I'm on the subject, what to make of Mrs Honour's strange behaviour? Anyone would think she was snooping around, just like me – but why? She can hardly want to clear Mr Draycott's name.*

Debo gave herself a little shake. *No time to think about that now – I can discuss it with Mummy and Nanny later. Right, where shall I search?* She thought for a second before deciding, *If the study is out, I'll go upstairs. Mrs Adams' bedroom is bound to be overflowing with clues.*

Feeling every inch the intrepid heroine, she crept out of the cupboard and began to tiptoe up the stairs. With the exception of one creaky step she made it to the top without mishap. One noisy step just added a delightful frisson of fear.

*Now which room was Mrs Adams' bedroom?*

The first door she tried was a cold white bathroom. Yet again she was struck with the contrast between the Adams' home and her own. At Farrington Hall, the bathrooms had pot plants on the windowsills, books galore and in Flora's there was even a gramophone record player and a stack of records.

The next door she opened revealed Mr Adams' dressing room. Debo only spared a cursory glance at Mr Adams' neat brash suits and shiny shoes.

It was when she opened the third door that she let out a quiet squeal. *Bingo!*

The double bed was modern with a matching pink satin headboard and quilted cover. The curtains were a garish blue and pink. In the window alcove was a mirrored dressing table that had a skirt of pleated material the same as the curtains. The dressing table boasted a sleek, modern silver brush-and-comb set. Hanging up on the wardrobe door was a pink silk negligee.

*Gosh! Gothic or what?* she thought with glee. She looked slowly around the room. *Where to start?* Her eyes rested on the dressing table. *That's probably the best spot for a clue or two.*

Creeping over, intent on exploring whether there were drawers behind the dressing table drapes, she paused to look at the photos in silver frames that nestled beside the brush-and-comb set. There was a wedding one, with Mrs Adams clutching a large bouquet. Even to Debo's young eyes it looked a bit sad; it was obviously a registry office and there were no guests. The neighbouring picture was a bit more interesting: a grainy image of a lacrosse team. The uniform was pre-war and sure enough, she spotted her mother looking unbelievably youthful. Smiling, she glanced at the only remaining photo, a small, skinny, knock-kneed boy looking up adoringly at a very beautiful young woman. Again, Debo guessed the age of the image from the clothes, the long skirt suggested it was a captured moment in time in the 1890s.

That was her last coherent thought before she felt a burning sensation around her mouth, the sickly smell of chloroform and all went black.

A little later at Farrington Hall, Debo's absence was noticed.

'I must admit that I am a little concerned,' confided Flora with a frown.

'About Debo?' clarified Nanny.

Flora nodded. 'It's not like her to miss a meal.' She frowned. 'I mean Tony is a totally different kettle of fish; he wouldn't eat at all if Mrs Wilkes didn't take him a sandwich now and again.'

Nanny commented, 'That woman spoils the boy – I saw her scurrying out to the garage with a tray today.'

'Tony seems determined to fix my Morgan.'

'I didn't know there was anything wrong with it.'

'Oh, there isn't, but he was so keen I didn't like to put the dampener on his enthusiasm.'

'Very wise, dear.' Nanny smiled with approval before suggesting, 'Why don't you go and ask Tony if he has seen her, and I'll check the house again.'

'Right oh!' agreed Flora.

With Dorothy trotting at her heels, she went to the boot room and pulled on her coat and boots before heading out to the garage. Anxiety added speed to her tread.

The maids, Mavis and Gladys, were just coming in, their cheeks rosy from the outside chill. They shook their heads when Flora asked them if they had seen Debo, so Flora continued walking to the garage.

Pushing the garage door open, she was surprised to see not only Tony, but Busby with a spanner in his hand. Dorothy was delighted by the discovery of her favourite human. With a lot of yapping and tail wagging, she threw herself at him. Order was only partly restored when he picked her up and allowed her to smother him with kisses. The garage was dimly lit and smelt strongly of oil and fumes.

In Dorothy's exuberance, she knocked his cap off. To Flora's mind, the revealing of Busby's unruly russet-coloured curls was rather appealing, but the sight of Busby and Tony engaged in a project side by side gave Flora a momentary jolt. *Roger would have loved to have been in here with his son, tinkering with an engine, but he never got the chance.* She caught a look of admiration in Tony's bright eyes as Busby handed him a rag and her stomach tightened. A familiar knot of sadness rendered her speechless for a second. *It should be Roger,* was her fleeting useless thought.

'Oh Mother, I forgot to mention that I arranged for Busby to come round this afternoon to lend a hand with the Morgan.'

'Lovely, darling. Do stay for tea, Busby.' She spoke automatically. *Why does one always offer tea when really one wants to cry?* Flora gathered her thoughts and added, 'Actually, it's probably a good thing you are here.'

Sensing Flora's serious mood, Busby hushed Dorothy and focused on Flora.

Flora swallowed. 'You see – Debo appears to be – well – missing.'

Busby took in Flora's unnaturally pinched expression. 'Are you sure?' he asked, his tone mild and considered.

Irritated beyond bearing by his comment, Flora snapped back, 'Of course I'm sure. I would hardly come in here and say, "Debo is missing" if I knew perfectly well that she was sitting in the library with a book and a box of chocolates.' She exhaled and regained a degree of composure. 'I came over here to ask Tony if he had any idea where she might have got to.'

Busby and Flora both looked at Tony. A pink flush crept up his face, starting at his collar and reaching the tips of his ears.

'Come on, Tony, tell us what you know,' Busby said with calm authority.

Tony's lanky frame drooped a little and his blue eyes scanned his mother's feet rather looking her in the face. Eventually he ran an oily hand through his mop of black hair and ventured a glance at Busby.

'Well,' he began hesitantly, 'she did mention wanting to search the Adams' house.'

Busby's brow furrowed. 'Why?'

'For clues,' explained Tony.

Busby rolled his eyes while Flora felt a wave of relief.

Nanny bustled in just in time to catch that part of their exchange and commented, 'That makes sense; her bicycle is missing.'

Flora smiled, her shoulders relaxed. 'Oh good, I'll just nip back to the house and ring them.'

Nanny and Busby exchanged a look.

'What?' asked Flora.

Nanny spoke slowly and quietly. 'I don't think that's a good idea.'

'Why ever not?' Flora was impatient to find her daughter and looked angrily at Nanny.

Unflappable, Nanny explained, 'My dear child, think about it. If Maud was murdered, there is a chance that the murderer is in the house.'

'And telephoning the house would only alert them and put Debo in danger?' Flora words came in a rush. She had an urge to flee but she didn't know where to. Her heart raced. She recognised that she was losing control but didn't know how to rein her spiralling emotions in. *Why didn't I listen to Debo when she wanted to talk to me? What if she's been hurt? What if she's frightened?*

She glanced around at the others. Tony had paled, Nanny's lips were set in a grim line and Busby was looking at her with concern.

Desperately she implored, 'So what are we meant to do? Just sit around here?'

Busby replied calmly, 'You and I can go there. I'll drive – you are not in a fit state to.'

They lost no time in setting off. Flora did not care for Busby being the one behind the wheel. *Why is the man driving so slowly? We may as well be walking.*

To make matters worse, he ignored all her urging to drive faster. She couldn't stop fidgeting with her hands and feet; sitting still in the car while Debo was missing was unbearable.

Flora's thoughts ranged from anger – *how could Debo be so irresponsible to go off like this?* – to despair – *how could I live without her?*

Eventually they arrived. Flora barely waited for the car to stop before she leapt from it and ran to the front door. She didn't knock, she just burst into the house, calling, 'Debo' at the top of her voice.

Her cries brought Derek Adams, Nurse Smythson and Mrs Scrubs all hurrying into the hall.

Busby was close on Flora's heels and took command. He spoke with calm authority as Derek Adams, Nurse Smythson and Mrs Scrubs all stared in amazement at them. 'Debo is missing and we have reason to believe she is here.'

Derek muttered, 'Oh dear, oh dear, but why would she come here?' He was dressed in outdoor wear and looked a little pale. He staggered and sat down heavily on a side chair. 'I'm so sorry, please excuse me. I took a turn around the garden and I am afraid I am not as strong as I thought I was. I haven't seen her.'

Mrs Scrubs had her sleeves rolled up, she wore an apron and

was red-faced. 'Well she's not in the washroom, I've been in there all morning, boiling the whites.'

Nurse Smythson was a little breathless. 'I haven't seen her either, but I've just come back from the bus stop. I'd hoped to go into Oxford but I missed the bus by a whisker.' Without removing her outdoor clothes, she calmly declared, 'We'd best set to and find her.' She gave Flora a businesslike smile, 'Try not to worry, Mrs Farrington. I am sure she can't have really disappeared; you know what girls of that age are like – always off on some adventure or other.'

Flora found the woman's composure reassuring. *Nurse Smythson is quite right, Debo is bound to be fine.*

'Now let's split up,' continued Nurse Smythson. 'I'll take the upstairs. Mrs Scrubs, would you kindly look in the kitchen area? Mr Adams, you don't look quite the thing. I think you had better sit for a little longer.'

Busby cleared his throat. 'I would prefer it if we all stuck together.' His voice brooked an authority that was not to be questioned.

Nurse Smythson momentarily met his gaze before saying, 'Very well, Inspector.'

Flora glanced at Busby. His face was passive but nonetheless Flora was aware of the subtext of his words. *Oh lord, he thinks one of them might be involved and he doesn't want to give them a chance to further harm Debo.*

The brief moment of hope Flora had experienced seconds before evaporated and once more her stomach knotted.

Her apprehension only grew with each room they searched. Idly she wondered why the house smelt like a hospital, or a dentist's office rather than a homely mixture of beeswax, lavender and baking.

Half an hour later she collapsed, defeated, into an armchair in the drawing room, Her shoulders slumped, she couldn't think straight and her breathing was tight.

She felt Busby's hand on her shoulder.

'What do we do now?' enquired Nurse Smythson in her matter-of-fact way.

'The child is obviously not here; we've searched everywhere,' commented Mrs Scrubs.

They looked at Busby for direction. 'If I might use your phone, Mr Adams?' he asked. 'I will call the police station.'

'Oh course, of course, the poor child. I wonder where she could have got to?'

As Busby was phoning Flora held her head in her hands. *Where oh where are you, Debo? Not the bedrooms, nor the outhouse – but where?* Flora mind rested on thoughts of Maud. *What if Debo has been murdered, just like Maud? Just like...*

She sprang to her feet, startling Busby, Nurse Smythson and Derek Adams. 'The lake! We haven't searched the lake.' She bolted for the door and seconds later she was outside and running for all she was worth towards the lake. It seemed to her there were acres of lawn to cross before she reached it.

Her lungs burned as she gasped for air. She was dimly aware of Busby close by, calling her name. She tore through the willows by the lake, ignoring the lash of their whip-thin branches on her bare cheeks. Her eyes remained on the lake; it looked serene and still while her thoughts were in turmoil.

She scanned the water. She could hear screams and was surprised to discover that it was her. 'Debo!' she wailed.

And then she saw a body – Debo's body – half in, half out of the water's edge. She wasn't shocked, she had expected to see her, but when she saw her limp, motionless body, all she could think was, *She is so small.*

Flora plunged into the icy water and dragged Debo fully onto the cold wet grass and rolled her onto her back. Her daughter's body was freezing.

She noticed that one of her shoes had come off. Knowing it was ridiculous, she thought of the old nursery rhyme, 'Diddle, diddle, dumpling'. The boy in that rhyme – *my son, John* – had had one shoe off and one shoe on, too.

Busby was on his knees beside her. He firmly pushed Flora to one side and set to work, forcing life back into Debo's body.

To Flora, the wait seemed like an eternity.

Busby was focused and calm as he rhythmically pumped Debo's arms above her head and back again. Debo's slight body looked so pathetic, like a rag doll rather than a robust girl with all her life in front of her, that Flora found it hard to watch.

Beads of sweat appeared on Busby's forehead. 'Come on, Debo!' he muttered.

Nurse Smythson appeared. She had her arms full of towels and rugs. She even had a small silver hip flask. She placed a rug around Flora's shoulders. Flora didn't have the energy to refuse it or shrug it off. In her distorted mind, she felt that if she suffered too, it would somehow help Debo.

Flora could hear a strange sound above the noise of the wind in the bare branches and the cawing of crows; she realised the sound was her own teeth chattering but she was powerless to stop.

Nurse Smythson pressed the hip flask to Flora's lips and as the burning spirit coursed down her throat Debo took her first spluttering breath.

Elation flooded Flora's body. She flung herself on her daughter, clutching her to her chest, crying and rocking her in her arms. Nurse Smythson dropped the flask and reached for the towel. Within seconds she was vigorously rubbing Debo's limbs with it, working around Flora.

Eventually, Flora glanced away from Debo and at Busby. He looked exhausted but was smiling. Their eyes met; Flora felt too much gratitude towards him that she could find the words to express it but as they looked into each other's eyes, words didn't seem to be needed.

# CHAPTER 10

*DISCUSSIONS*

Later on, Debo was tucked up with a hot water bottle, a multitude of rugs and the Farrington Hall library fire blazing. Dr Honour had already been, had applied some soothing ointment to where the chloroform had stung her face and declared her fit as a fiddle, a sentiment Nanny had concurred with as the child devoured the meal she served on a tray.

Now all that was left was for Flora to remonstrate, 'What do you mean, you don't have a clue who attacked you? You must have some idea! Was it a man or a woman?'

Debo, who had moved on to a cup of tea and a generous slice of cake, shrugged her shoulders as she finished her mouthful. 'Couldn't say.'

Exasperated, Flora sighed. 'Honestly, darling, you are our first concrete clue and you are not coming up with any useful information.'

Unperturbed, Debo took another mouthful of cake, swallowed and queried, 'I say, Mummy, aren't you meant to be prostate with relief that I didn't die, rather than suggesting I wasn't very observant?'

Flora helped herself to some cake. 'Well of course, Debo, I was quite, quite distraught, wasn't I, Busby?'

'Quite,' concurred Busby dryly.

Flora continued, 'I even plunged into the lake without giving my new suede boots a second thought. Let me assure you that greater love hath no woman than she lay down her new footwear for another.' She sipped her tea. 'But that was then and this is now.'

Nanny, who was sitting in an armchair close by the fire knitting, commented, 'Rather than bickering about what the child didn't see, let's look at what you and Busby noticed about possible suspects in the Adams' house.'

Busby spoke first. 'Mr Adams admits he had been in the grounds and seemed exhausted; perhaps too exhausted for having just strolled around his garden.'

Flora came as close to rolling her eyes as a lady could permit herself. 'Do lay off the poor man, Busby. He's just lost his wife and was visibly distressed when we told him about Debo. Besides which, as I have said before, he's a lamb. Now that Nurse Smythson, with all her clipped efficiency, would be more than capable of killing off any number of people. She was definitely flushed when we arrived. We only have her word for it that it was because she'd been running for a bus rather than trying to drown Debo.'

'Then there's Mrs Scrubs,' put in Nanny, without looking up from her knitting. 'Flora mentioned she was red faced, with her sleeves rolled up and her apron on. Pretending you've been doing the washing would make an excellent excuse for doing a spot of drowning.'

Debo frowned. 'But that can't be right.'

'Whatever not, darling?' Flora was pleased to see the colour had returned to Debo's cheeks and better still she seemed to be coming up with some thoughtful sleuthing ideas.

'Because when I saw her, she was inside doing the silver.'

Flora tilted her head on one side and regarded her daughter. 'Sorry, I'm not making the connection.'

'Well by the time you have stoked the boiler and collected the laundry it's an all-day affair and you certainly don't embark on silver polishing. Besides, surely, they use Dills Laundry like everyone else in the village with more than a ha'penny to their name.'

'The child has a point,' agreed Nanny.

Debo smiled and glowed a little with pride. 'Ooh!' she suddenly squealed with delight. 'I forgot to tell you – Mrs Scrubs isn't a wizened old woman at all.'

'She isn't?' asked Flora, thinking of her long-gone pet tortoise.

'I caught her unawares; she was cuddling her cat and honestly she looked pretty.' She looked around at Flora's, Busby's and Nanny's disbelieving countenances. 'And what's more her hair is long with a curl to it and there is even a hint of ginger among the grey – oh, *and* she can sing.'

Flora frowned with concern. 'Darling, did you also have a bang on the head?'

'Concussion can affect the memory,' commented Nanny.

'Really! I come up with some juicy new info and you don't even believe me.'

'Any other suggestions?' asked Busby. 'Not about Mrs Scrubs but other suspects.'

From the comfort of the sofa, Debo added, 'Well, don't forget Mrs Honour – she was skulking around.'

Flora frowned, thinking about Debo's earlier description of Mrs Honour's behaviour at the Adams' house. 'Um, don't you think you might have been mistaken? You must have misinterpreted Mrs Honour's actions.'

Debo snorted. 'Misinterpreted? Really, Mummy! How can one misinterpret Mrs Honour hiding in the study at the sound of Nurse Smythson's voice?'

No one queried her statement and Busby made a mental note to question the lady later. Satisfied with the response, Debo lifted her chin and straightened herself. 'It's crystal clear that I was attacked because I was about to find some vital clue.' She flushed with pride and pleasure. 'So, even if we don't know who exactly attempted to murder me, this puts Mr Draycott in the clear. After all, he was under lock and key.'

Busby spoke quietly. 'Not exactly; it just means we know he didn't attack you. We still have no evidence he didn't murder Mrs Adams.'

Debo pouted a little sulkily, and said, 'It's not exactly likely that there is more than one murderous villain running around the village.'

Nanny and Flora both nodded but Busby was noncommittal.

'Have some more cake,' suggested Flora, offering her daughter another slice.

Debo had a mouthful and rallied. Looking at Busby, she enquired, 'Alright, but shouldn't you be investigating other suspects?'

Busby raised an eyebrow. 'Like who?'

Debo thought for a moment. 'What about the angels that a lot of villagers saw the day, or rather the night, that Mrs Adams was murdered?'

Flora sighed. 'Darling, I really don't think we can blame the heavenly host for Maud's demise.'

'In that case we just need to do a spot more investigating.' Debo smiled, evidently happy at the prospect.

Busby immediately took a firm hand. 'Absolutely not! I will not have you putting yourself in danger and butting into police business.'

Debo pursed her lips and glared defiantly at him.

Flora deftly broke the tension. 'Don't take it personally, darling,' she said to her daughter. 'He is always a total killjoy when it comes to sleuthing.' Turning her most dazzling smile on Busby, she asked, 'More cake?'

When Busby left Farrington Hall, he went straight to quiz Mrs Honour. Her meagre fire and cake made him long for the bounty and warmth of Flora's library. Mrs Honour herself was just as cold and unwelcoming as her drawing room.

To Busby's question, she raised an imperious eyebrow and looked down her nose at him with distaste. 'I realised that I had lost an earring. I recalled that the last time I had worn the earrings was when I had visited Maud a week before she died. We sat in her study and discussed the upcoming fireworks party.'

'Why didn't you alert Mr Adams to your presence?'

Mrs Honour look of distaste morphed to disgust. 'The poor man has just lost his wife; I am not so insensitive as to bother him over such a trivial matter.'

'And did you find it?' Busby scrutinised Mrs Honour; she was not an easy woman to read beyond her obvious dislike for him. He thought, *She would be a formidable poker player.*

Her smile didn't reach her eyes. 'Yes, I am wearing them now.'

As Busby drove away, he thought, *well that was inconclusive.* His mind went dwelling on all the time he had wasted on the phone to the London records offices, *all inconclusive too.* They seemed to be having problems tracing both Derek's and Mrs Scrubs birth certificates, *but I doubt it means much more than there is a normal level of incompetence.* He had deliberately not shared this piece of information with Flora as he knew she would have been straight off to confront them both about their missing documentation. He did have qualms about not having told her about all he had discovered about Nurse Smythson's unhappy past, but as he reasoned, *Flora is a civilian and not a police officer.* The question marks he had around the inhabitants of Maud's old home had fuelled his insistence that he and Flora should go straight there in search of Debo and not phone ahead. He smiled, *at least Debo is home and safe.*

Back at Farrington Hall, they found that news of Debo's adventures had spread swiftly around the village. Mrs Scrubs had an advantage over other folk as she had been there when the child was found. She was a surprise early visitor.

'I've brought some sweets for the girl,' she told Flora sourly. It was more as if she was announcing an unfortunate outbreak of plague rather than a thoughtful gift for an invalid.

Flora smiled and tried to banish her thoughts of Mrs Scrubs' resemblance to her pet tortoise and imagine Debo's description of a Mrs Scrubs that was pretty, singing, and bountifully blessed by hair. She failed and said, 'How kind. Do come in, Debo is up and about – she's bounced back brilliantly. I'll call her.'

'No need for that!' Mrs Scrubs said hastily as she thrust a brown paper bag into Flora's hands. She turned on her heels and marched off.

Flora took the sweets into the library where Debo was holding court. The two beautiful boys, Pierre and Anton, were handing her two stunning bouquets of flowers. She accepted them with a becoming blush. Flora gave an inner sigh. *It won't be many more years before she has troops of dashing young men lining up to give her flowers.*

Gigi, who was looking fabulous in a knitted two-piece, handed over a couple of books. 'One is a bit of romance with just enough spice to make a young girl's heart flutter, and the other is about Victorian female explorers. A girl needs more adventure in her life than just a burning love.'

'More gifts for you,' announced Flora, proffering the bag of sweets. 'Mrs Scrubs just dropped these off for you.'

'Gosh, that's jolly decent. Aunt Gigi, I saw Mrs Scrubs with her hair down when she was playing with her cat. She was singing and she is actually pretty!'

'How intriguing,' said Gigi, pursing her brightly lipsticked lips but the soft laughter lines around her bright blue eyes crinkled mischievously.

'She dances beautifully too!' murmured Anton.

Flora stared. 'You've seen her dancing?'

Anton appeared not to hear.

Gigi said, 'I need to meet this lady, she sounds interesting.'

'Well good luck with that – she tends to keep herself to herself.'

'Oh and she tells lies,' commented Debo.

Flora leaned forward. 'Do tell.'

'Little lies – unnecessary pointless ones. I've been thinking about it ever since she told you she was doing the laundry when I saw her polishing the silver. It's sort of stirred up several old memories. Last hols when I was having a good old bike ride, I overheard her telling a neighbour that she had just been to the post office when I had seen her go in the opposite direction. And saying she never eats cake when I was amazed at the last village fête by how quickly she swallowed down a slice of Victoria sponge. It's not as if they were the sort of things to make her seem more important than she is.'

Nanny looked up from her knitting. 'Which reminds me, on the day of the funeral she told me she came from the Lake District or was it Wales? Then she said it was Ireland. And as for her supposed dead husband, she told me he was a butcher and a bit later he was a clerk. If you ask me, there never was a husband.'

Gigi drew her eyebrows together and tilted her head on one side as she pondered this information. Eventually she commented, 'That must have been dangerous.'

'Dangerous how?' asked Flora.

'Being someone who tells lies and living under the same roof as someone who liked to collect secrets.'

'So you think she should go to the top of the Murdering Maud suspect list?'

'Not necessarily. Just because someone tells lies, it doesn't mean they might be a murderer.'

'Quite right!' declared Debo with feeling. 'Mummy is always telling lies and she isn't a murderer.'

Flora almost dropped the teacup she had in her hand. Somehow, she managed to replace it on the saucer with a loud rattle but no breakages. 'Darling! Whatever do you mean?'

She could see both Nanny and Gigi were grinning, which only heightened Flora's discomfort.

'Only the other day you told Mrs Wilkes that her treacle pudding was delicious, when I saw you feed it to Dorothy when Mrs Wilkes wasn't around,' explained Debo.

Flora had to concede this point. 'And it made the poor dear sick.' She gave Dorothy an apologetic tummy rub. 'Actually, I didn't say it was delicious, I only said it was just like Nanny used to make.' All eyes turn to Nanny and her knitting. 'And you know what a filthy cook Nanny is.'

Nanny simply smiled. 'All part of being a good nanny, me dear. It's not good for young things to eat too many sweet things.'

Gigi chuckled. 'And well done, Debo, you have admirably demonstrated that a moral failing does not necessarily lead to being a murderer.'

# CHAPTER II

### A BREAKDOWN

By the next day Debo was fully recovered and keen to go to Oxford. Tony surprised Flora by announcing he wished to go, too.

'But you loathe shopping at the best of times, let alone at Christmas?' she said.

'I want to visit Blackwell's; they have some engineering books,' he explained through a mouthful of toast and marmalade.

They loaded themselves in the Rolls Royce and headed off, wrapped up warmly for the cold journey. The car was big and heavy to drive but Flora insisted on not having a chauffeur. 'Yet another person to bother with,' she would say if anyone queried her decision. This was only partly true as another reason was she got car sick if she wasn't driving.

They made fairly good progress. Flora was enjoying herself as she and Debo sang Christmas carols, with Tony occasionally joining in. The back roads were poor but once they hit the main road Flora was able to speed up – that was until they found out traffic had been halted by an overturned cart in the road that was totally blocking it both in and out of Oxford. Judging by the number of men milling around and shouting instructions, it didn't look as if it would be cleared any time soon.

'Never mind,' declared Flora, 'I know a shortcut.'

She turned the car down a small twisting lane, which had a great many potholes. But twists and potholes were soon the least of her worries. The engine began to splutter, and Flora could feel it losing power until eventually with a pop and a wheeze it stopped altogether.

Elated Tony announced, 'Don't worry, Mother; I'm sure I can fix it.'

He leapt from the car and had the bonnet up in a trice, leaving Flora to sigh and suggest to Debo, 'Come on, darling, let's see if that house has a telephone so we can ring for help. If not, I fear we may be spending Christmas in the wilds of Oxfordshire.'

They began picking their way up the muddy lane towards a low and long, thatched dwelling. There was a hopeful plume of smoke rising from the chimney.

'My shoes are going to be ruined – the second pair in a matter of days,' muttered Flora. 'This would never have happened if we had been in the Morgan.'

Debo was more practical. 'But how would we all have fitted in it? Tony could hardly have perched on the bonnet all the way to Oxford.'

'True,' conceded Flora.

'Goodness, what a lot of children,' commented Debo as they got closer to the house.

There were a great many children, ranging in age from toddlers to those who seemed almost ready to be out working. All were well clad in sturdy boots and warm woollies. At the sight of Flora and Debo they gave out a whoop and would have overwhelmed them if a small, round, elderly lady had not emerged from the doorway and called them off. Laughing, she bid the children to go back to their games and welcomed her unexpected guests with a warm smile.

'I do believe, we have stumbled upon the original old lady who lived in a shoe and had so many children she didn't know what to do,' whispered Flora, making Debo giggle.

Once inside, the pair were greeted with a sense of warmth and happiness. The house smelt of baking and beeswax. Homemade Christmas decorations brightened every possible corner. The lady introduced herself as Mrs Pie. Flora detected a faint whiff of extra strong mints. *Evidently, a lady with a sweet tooth.*

'So sorry to intrude,' apologised Flora, 'but we have broken down and were wondering if you had a telephone so we could ring a garage?'

Mrs Pie's eyes twinkled as she laughed. 'Why, we don't have anything like that, but I can ask a couple of the older boys to nip along the road and get Farmer Harris to phone for you.'

'That would be most kind. I say, is this a school?'

Again, Mrs Pie let out a rich laugh. 'Why, bless you, no. 'Tis better than any school. It's a home for myself and any young 'un who finds themselves without kin.' She beamed at Flora and Debo. 'As I often say, I am the luckiest lady that ever lived. Just look at all the wonderful children that I have been blessed with.' She indicated a wall of photos.

'Goodness, what a wonderful display,' exclaimed Flora looking at an array of photos of different children, all shapes and sizes and in their Sunday best. Some of the photos were old enough to be sepia. The children were mostly smiling, but some looked a little uncertain.

Mrs Pie's round face creased into a broad smile. 'Less a rogues' gallery and more my flight of angels.'

Debo stepped forward to better scrutinise the images. 'Gosh, Mummy, that one is a dead ringer for Nanny.' She pointed to a faded sepia photo of a chubby child, with chaotic curls, a pug face and small hedgehog eyes.

Flora laughed, nodding her agreement. She too, took a closer look at the portraits. 'And this could be a young Mrs Honour.' She regarded a girl of about twelve, pinch-faced but beautiful, with sharp assessing eyes. Even in the photo she appeared to be looking down her nose at them all.

Mrs Pie was at her side. She sighed. 'Poor Carrie – a troubled soul. She always was rather bossy and had an unattractive habit of considering herself better than others. She hasn't kept in touch.'

'That sounds about right,' laughed Debo. She stepped closer to take a better look at a small portrait of a little boy. He looked into the camera, knock-kneed and unsure. Debo stared and pointed. 'That's the little boy I saw in Mr Adams' bedroom with the beautiful lady. You remember, Mummy, I told you about the photo in the silver frame he had by his bed.'

Mrs Pie beamed. 'That's a special boy. Jeremiah Fisher or

I should say Captain Jeremiah Fisher, of the Royal Navy. He always calls in when he's home on leave. He is that handsome in his uniform – let me show you his latest photo.'

She scuttled from the room, all thoughts of boys summoning help forgotten. Flora decided to make the best of it and pointed at a tiny child and exclaimed, 'Look darling! A juvenile tortoise if ever I saw one, Mrs Scrubs to a T – apart from the hair. That child has the most luxuriant curls but Mrs Scrubs has a bun.'

Debo felt compelled to gently admonish her mother. 'Mummy, you can't call people animals – it's not kind.'

'No, dear, you are quite right, but in my defence, it could be taken as a compliment as I generally like tortoises.' Flora had already moved onto the next portrait. With a grin she commented, 'Now this girl looks like a character.'

Debo regarded the skinny girl who beamed out of the faded photo. She agreed with a nod. 'She does look frightfully jolly.'

Mrs Pie bustled in with a large black photo frame in her hand. Overhearing Debo's words, she smiled broadly, 'She is! Even now she never stops smiling and laughing. Would you believe she grew up to marry a lord?'

Flora was about to comment when Tony stuck his head through door with a jovial, 'All sorted.'

Flora glanced at her watch. 'Well done, darling! Oxford will be heaving with Christmas shoppers, but we will still have plenty of time.'

Mrs Pie put the photo on the side, sensing that Flora was keen to be off. 'Well, you must be away but do call in next time you are passing.'

# CHAPTER 12

## *CHRISTMAS SHOPPING IN OXFORD*

Mrs Honour had thought that taking Lady Clarke shopping in Oxford and then meeting Victor for tea was the perfect way to spend the day, but now she wasn't so sure. She had hoped that the grandeur and history of the colleges, not to mention the famous Bodleian Library, would impress her but it was not to be so.

'Amanda, darling, I simply don't know how you bear it,' sighed Lady Clarke. Amanda Honour, who was stiff and brittle at the best of times, tensed. She felt she knew what was coming.

'How anyone can do their Christmas shopping in this little place is beyond me.' She waved a bored hand in the general direction of Oxford's dreamy spires.

With a gracious smile, Mrs Honour assured her, 'I do go up to Town quite often. The train is so easy.'

Lady Clarke sighed again. 'Oh, London is all very well but, personally, I prefer Paris or New York.' She pulled her fur trim coat a little tighter around her. She flicked her gaze over to her older companion who was clad in a blue tweed with co-ordinating hat. 'Which do you prefer?'

Deliberately Mrs Honour paused, apparently focusing her cold grey eyes on a shop window full of the most delicious-looking chocolate, decorated with red ribbon and holly sprigs. 'Sorry, dear, I was distracted by this rather attractive window display.' She indicated the enchanting chocolates. 'What did you say?'

'Which city do you prefer: New York or Paris?'

Mrs Honour, ever the master of deception, smiled. She felt calm, assured in her ability to generally mislead this young woman. Mrs Honour had never been to either but knew that the appearance of being well travelled was important. 'I think both have their own charms, but naturally, their real attraction lies in the intellectual riches of their museums and galleries rather than their shops.'

This silenced Lady Clarke, as Mrs Honour knew it would. With a single remark she had firmly established herself as having the intellectual and perhaps even the moral high ground. They wandered a little further along.

Hierarchy established, Mrs Honour could afford to be gracious. She smiled at Lady Clarke. 'Now, my dear, I really must choose a gift for Victor. What do you think of that tie?' She pointed at blue one the shop window.

Lady Clarke crinkled her pert little nose. 'It would rather bring out the colour of his eyes.' She exhaled. 'I have no idea what to get him. Men are so difficult to buy gifts for, aren't they?'

Mrs Honour nodded while bestowing a conspiratorial smile. 'You need have no fear. Victor is so besotted with you, he will adore anything you give him.'

'Really?' A small frown lined her brow. Suddenly she was less the sophisticated traveller and more the young woman suffering the pangs of unrequited love. 'He's so reserved, though. I find it impossible to know what he is thinking.' Her frown deepened and she bit her lip. 'Sometimes, I think he doesn't care for me at all.'

Mrs Honour let out a tight laugh. 'Typical man, I'm afraid. They are so coy about expressing their true emotions.' With her gloved hand, she patted the young woman on the arm. 'Let me assure you that when I am alone with him he can talk of nothing else but how much he adores you.' She paused for emphasis and even raised an eyebrow. 'And, dare I say it, he has mentioned more than once how much he is looking forward to setting up home and his new practice in the heart of London – with you.'

'Really?' Lady Clarke brightened. 'He's never even hinted at marriage to me. In that case I will get him a tiepin to go with your gift.'

Mrs Honour felt satisfied; a tiepin was a good counterpoint to the generous present she had secretly secured for Victor to 'gift' to Lady Clarke. She could easily imagine the young woman's elation when she would receive the extremely expensive earrings she had already wrapped.

Lady Clarke's mind had obviously been put at ease, as she was all smiles as they entered the store.

'What was your wedding like?' she asked Mrs Honour as they came back out onto the street. Her tone was almost careless, perhaps even uninterested, but it sent Mrs Honour's heart beating and her mind racing for ways to cloak the reality of her own wedding in fabrication. The younger woman continued wistfully, 'I want something frightfully grand. I plan on being married at Hanover Square, with acres of flowers and yards of silk and all my friends and family there.'

The thought of herself as a central figure in such a grand social event made Mrs Honour's stony heart actually beat even faster with a rare feeling of happiness. In this elated state, it was easy for her to brush over her own shameful wedding day. Only two witnesses had been the guests at the shabby registry office. Victor's father's family had refused to attend. Mrs Honour thought that this had been natural enough; they had disapproved of her background and even more to the growing child in her belly.

The pregnancy had been unfortunate but necessary. How else would she have been able to secure marriage to a man as wealthy and well connected as Victor's father?

'Every girl feels like a princess on her wedding day,' she said lightly, then truthfully, she added, 'It was the happiest day of my life.' Her euphoria on that day had been less to do with the groom and more to do with the marriage certificate being her passport to a world of security and social respect.

Lady Clarke wasn't really listening; her thoughts were still on herself. 'At least it will be more fun than being presented.'

Mrs Honour was used to dodging all mention of being presented to the monarch, that age-old courtly rite of passage had been far outside her humble youth. She simply smiled and nodded, implying but not actually stating that she knew it all too well from her own experience.

Nurse Smythson was enjoying her trip to Oxford. She only had a few pennies to spare, but then, as she told herself philosophically, she didn't have many people to buy gifts for. *I would like to get something for Derek, though.* Mentally she checked herself. *Mr Adams.*

Feeling happy but a little tired she stopped outside a tearoom. It was nestled down a winding side street. The cobbles in front of it and the small paned window could all be straight out of Dickens. She checked her purse and counted the coppers. *Just enough for a pot of tea and perhaps a mince pie.*

The tearoom was busy but it smelt wonderfully of Christmas spices, and the waitress was cheery and helpfully found Nurse Smythson the last table.

*How fortunate I am,* thought Nurse Smythson. *And it's by the window too.*

Dr Honour was not feeling in the least bit fortunate. He had come into Oxford to discuss Paul Draycott's case with a colleague; he hoped they might be able to build a medical argument to mitigate his sentence.

The day had begun badly with his mother discovering his plans and insisting that she and Lady Clarke should all drive in together and then meet at The Randolph Hotel for tea.

The journey in had been unpleasant, with him enduring the two women's constant high-pitched bitchy chatter. His meeting had finished with no real results, and he was already dreading tea, followed by the drive home in his mother's and Lady Clarke's company.

So, when he spotted the two women on the street in front of him, he looked around for an escape route. Seeing the door to the tearoom, he took swift evasive action.

He had thought he would just hide inside for a moment and

give them time to pass before he left, but when he looked up he saw Nurse Smythson.

She was smiling. He flushed as he realised her amusement was the result of her having watched his evasive action from her window seat. He was surprised when she offered him the seat at her table. He hesitated and then joined her, unaware that Nurse Smythson was as surprised as he was by her suggestion he should join her.

They had never really had a chance to speak to each other outside their professional roles. He had been grateful for her calm efficiency during Mrs Adams' emergency appendix operation, *It was a stroke of good fortune that she had been in the area and that Mrs Ford had rung to tell me about the experienced surgical nurse who was just finishing a local private nursing contract.* He had thought her an excellent nurse during Mrs Adams initial days post operative but then…*What had happened to the missing morphine?*

The embarrassment of the situation was partly eased by the necessity of ordering tea and mince pies. After a while Dr Honour felt bold enough to ask, 'Do you actually enjoy Christmas?'

A little taken back by the abruptness of the question, Nurse Smythson thought about it, then replied, 'I used to.' When she smiled, all traces of weariness left her eyes. Dr Honour was struck by how she looked so different as she recalled happier times. 'My father always prided himself on finding the biggest, bushiest Christmas tree possible.' She laughed. 'One year he got it totally wrong and the tip of the tree was bent over by the ceiling. We had an awful job fixing the star to the top.'

Dr Honour was surprised by how much he liked the sound of her laughter, it was light and joyous. 'And your mother?'

'She died when I was so very young that she is not even a hazy memory.' Her voice and expression were neutral.

'I'm sorry – how sad.'

She gave him a slight smile. 'I know this sounds odd, but growing up, I didn't notice her absence; my father was so wonderful he really filled every corner of my life. He was always waiting for me at the school gates.' She laughed again. 'He listened with such regard to all my daily doings that I really believed I was the most fascinating little lady that had ever lived.' Her eyes sparkled and even her mouth lost its tightness. The fine lines on her brow softened. 'He had supper with me every night. In the evenings we both loved playing the piano together or reading in front of the fire.' She threw him a mischievous look. 'Can you imagine we read *The Secret Garden* cover to cover four times? It was years later that I learnt he was only able to spend all that time with me because he would work through the night after I went to sleep.'

Dr Honour smiled. 'And do you still get to spend time with him?'

Now her face darkened, and she looked down at her napkin. 'I'm afraid that he is no longer with us.'

Dr Honour stammered feeling at a loss for what to say. 'Oh, I am so sorry.' To his mind, the words were trite and inadequate.

She glanced up at him and he was taken aback by the look of desperation behind her eyes. A hard line creased between her eyes and he noticed her hand were fists. Her voice was hushed and rapid. 'The awful thing is, he didn't die naturally.'

Dr Honour found himself leaning forwards and whispering too. 'The war?'

'If only!' she spat out angrily. 'He was a victim of his own kind heart.' Then so quietly that Dr Honour could barely hear, she said, 'He took his own life.'

Silence ensued. He couldn't find any words. After a moment or two, he reached out his hand and laid it on hers.

There were tears in her eyes when she looked up at him. 'He couldn't bear the shame; he didn't love me enough. Overnight, I lost him, my home, my comfortable lifestyle – and why? All because he had been foolish enough to trust a man without scruples as his business partner. A man who was happy to profit while supplying sub-standard boots to poor boys fighting in the trenches. That man walked away wealthier than ever, leaving my father to bear all the blame.

He squeezed her hand; compassion was an inadequate word to express his feelings towards Nurse Smythson.

Suddenly, she gave herself a little visible shake, as if she could simply shake off all the heartbreak. She withdrew her hand and once more she was hard and crisp. 'And so I became a nurse.'

'And a good one,' put in Dr Honour, feeling the loss of her hand beneath his.

'Thank you.' There was a pause before she continued, 'But enough about me. Tell me about yourself.'

He shrugged. 'Nothing much to tell.'

'Oh come now! You must have dreams and ambitions.'

He toyed with his cake, debating whether to tell her. He gazed up at her face. The traces of vulnerability were gone, but they had been there – he had seen them. Feeling as if he was diving off a cliff into the unknown, he admitted, 'I would like to open a nursing home for men with shellshock.' He looked at her steadily, fearful of her reaction. Even within the medical profession shellshock was often seen as a pseudo-medical term for cowardice.

As he watched, a light came into her eyes. 'What a wonderful ambition,' she said. 'Do tell me more about how you would run it. I have read some of Medical Officer Charles Myers on the subject.'

They talked on for hours as time slipped away. Fresh tea was brought and Dr Honour forgot all about his mother, Lady Clarke and The Randolph.

Flora was not enjoying shopping in Oxford. *So much for dreamy spires, I just wish the pavements were wider or that there were less shoppers. That's the second person who has trodden on my toes. St Aldate's is full to overflowing. Thank goodness the children wanted to do their own things and meet up later for tea, so I don't have them to worry about as well as these ghastly crowds.* Everyone seemed to be as fraught and overburdened with their Christmas shopping duties as Flora was.

She battled her way down Cornmarket Street with all the crowds of people. *Why do I always leave my Christmas shopping until the last minute? I always have such good intentions of having everything bought and wrapped by November, yet somehow I always end up by doing a last-minute dash.* It was at this point in her musings that she literally bumped into a fellow purchaser.

'Oh, I am so sorry,' she began and then realised it was Busby, and she wasn't really sorry at all. His gentle good looks became more and more appealing to Flora every time she saw him. Smiling up at him she enquired, 'Christmas shopping?'

'Only partly. I had to come into Oxford on police matters but thought I would just pop in and pick up a couple of things. As it happens, I have remarkably few people to buy Christmas presents for.'

'Isn't that wonderful!'

Busby raised an eyebrow. 'It is?'

Flora beamed. 'Yes! Because I have far too many people to buy for and you can help me.'

Busby titled his head on one side and gave her a quizzical look. 'Seriously?'

She was quick to assure him, 'I never joke about food or Christmas shopping.' She put a companionable arm through his. 'You are not on duty or anything tiresome like that, are you?'

He shook his head. 'Not as of twenty minutes ago.'

'Now what should I get for Nanny?'

'Nanny is easy: a bottle of excellent whisky and a box of fine cigars.'

Flora pulled a face. 'But that's what I get her every year.'

'And I bet she is always delighted.'

Flora nodded and laughed.

Actually, she laughed a good deal over the next couple of hours. When she thought about it later, she couldn't quite recall what had been so amusing. *I do find him easy company,* she mused, *and it's so nice to be able to spend time with him without having to compete with Dorothy for his attention.* One way and another the time flew by.

Beaumont Street was just as overflowing with people as the rest of Oxford. There were people of every age, size and condition, although Flora fancied there was a higher proportion of grandmothers and babies in prams than was necessary. She was trying to make way for one such grandmother who was proudly, if slowly, pushing a pram when she unwittingly stepped into the road just as a red bus was passing. Flora heard the horn and swinging around saw the whites of the terrified driver's eyes. A woman in the crowd let out a scream. Before she had time to have her rather adventurous life flash before her eyes, she felt Busby's reassuringly strong arms wrap around her and her many parcels. He pulled her to safety. It all happened so quickly that she missed the sensation of terror and went straight to enjoying being pressed against his chest. All she could think was, *'Gosh!'*

It was with reluctance that Flora found her own feet. She straightened her hat and checked her parcels, then smiled. 'All's well.'

He laughed. 'You really do need me at your side permanently.'

'Well, Dorothy would love that,' acknowledged Flora. She gazed down at her various bags and parcels and passed them to Busby. 'Now, we have got gifts for everyone but you.'

His eyes widened; for once he was unsure. He stammered, 'No need.'

'I insist.' She smiled, then to lighten the intensity of the mood she asked, 'What shall it be? A tie? A hip flask? A pet python?'

He considered the matter. 'I have a tie, and I don't want a python so let's make it a hip flask.'

'Good. Solid silver.'

'I'd rather have steel.'

Flora paused, 'Steel? That reeks of the industrial rather than…' She stopped herself before she said, 'Romance.'

He didn't seem to have noticed. 'It's impressively strong,' he explained.

She felt a girlish quiver as she thought, *Like you!*

Swiftly regaining a sense of propriety, Flora glanced at her watch. 'Goodness, look at the time. The children will be chomping at the trough – or rather their tea-table at The Randolph.'

From behind a precarious pile of parcels, Busby heartily agreed.

They arrived at the hotel and allowed the cloakroom girl to take charge of both their gifts and coats. The hotel was delightfully warm and boasted a jolly Christmas tree in the lobby and a roaring fire in the tearoom.

The place was heaving with weary shoppers including Mrs Honour and Lady Clarke. Neither lady appeared to be particularly thrilled about unexpectedly meeting Flora. *But then I don't think those two are ever particularly thrilled about anything in their lives.* Mrs Honour gave Busby a narrow-eyed and meaningful stare, which he easily ignored.

Bidding Mrs Honour and Lady Clarke as gracious a greeting as she could muster, Flora was delighted to spot Debo and Tony seated by a window. By the look of the steaming tea pot and the sandwiches and mince pies awaiting them on attractive stands, they had been sensible enough to order the tea and not wait for Flora to arrive.

They greeted Busby affably and showed none of Mrs Honour's shocked surprise at their mother having acquired a policeman.

Flora had only had the time to enjoy one fortifying cup of tea when they were interrupted by a rather beautiful, willowy and very young lady. She had golden hair, a fresh complexion and wore a beautifully cut and impeccably understated outfit.

Busby was on his feet immediately and the smiles they exchanged were warm enough to quite put Flora off her tea. She had never quite worked out how old he was but she guessed he was a year or two younger than her, while this lady was definitely several years Busby's junior. *That would make her decades younger than me,* thought Flora, *which makes her little more than a child – gauche and uninteresting.* She tried hard not to look at her sophisticated costume or manner, but eventually she had to admit, *well perhaps not gauche just—*

As she struggled for the word, Tony, murmured, 'Gorgeous.' Flora glanced at him and noticed he was staring at the new arrival with open-mouthed admiration.

'Jacqueline,' declared Busby, embracing her and exchanging a kiss on each cheek. 'You must allow me to introduce you to everyone. Mrs Farrington, may I present Mademoiselle Jacqueline Bernard?'

As they shook hands, Jacqueline looked Flora in the eye and said, '*Enchanté.*'

For the first time in her life Flora wished the French accent wasn't so appealing. She gave a stiff smile as she enquired, 'And how do you two know each other?'

Jacqueline gave an attractive tinkling laugh. 'Our mothers were friends.' She looked coquettishly up at Busby. *Surely those long lashes can't be natural? And why is she standing so close to him?* 'Would you believe when I was a little girl, I was madly in love with him. I used to dream that one day I would grow up to be a beautiful lady and he would return my affection.'

Busby had the grace to colour. Flora's eyes narrowed as she looked from one to the other.

Debo broke the ensuing silence as she stated matter-of-factly, 'Sounds a bit soppy to me.'

Jacqueline looked at Debo, confused. 'Soppy? What is this word? I am not familiar with it.'

Flora stepped in and tartly explained, 'She means, pathetic, spineless and insipid.'

Debo looked at her mother in surprise. 'Not exactly Mummy. I meant, just a bit wet.'

Jacqueline smiled. 'Well, I mustn't disturb you any longer, but don't worry, Claudius, we will be seeing a lot of each other in the future.'

'We will?' queried Busby.

'*Mais oui*! I believe you live very close to Colonel and Mrs Ford?' Busby nodded and her smile broadened. 'I am their new governess. I didn't write and tell you because I wanted to be your *petite surprise de Noël.*'

Crisply Flora murmured, 'How lovely. Busby was only recently lamenting he didn't have anyone to buy Christmas gifts for.'

Debo looked keenly at Busby. 'Claudius? Is that your first name? Gosh, poor you! I bet you got ruthlessly bullied at school. With a handle like that no wonder you like to go by simply, "Busby".'

Jacqueline smiled. 'I really must go; Mrs Ford is beckoning me.' She looked over to where a matronly woman was sitting with three neat daughters, all in matching dresses and plaited hair. 'But this is but the briefest of adieus rather than a goodbye.'

'It is?' queried Flora.

'*Mais oui*! I believe, Mrs Farrington, that you are kind enough to be hosting the Lords and Ladies Ball?'

Reluctantly Flora nodded.

'Naturally, as the Ford's governess, I will be attending.' She turned the radiance of her smile on Busby. 'I have the most divine dress to wear and Claudius, you must promise to save me one,' here Flora noticed she pursed her rosebud lips, '*ou plusieurs danses pour moi.*'

Busby seemed to be struggling to speak.

Tony muttered, 'Good-oh.'

Deciding to help, Flora said crisply, 'My, won't that be jolly? I'm sure, dear old Claudius would love to dance the night away with you, but he will be very busy helping.'

'With what?' asked Debo.

'Oh, just things,' said Flora airily. 'Now, mademoiselle, I can see that Mrs Ford is getting ready to leave so I will say goodbye.'

Flora put just enough emphasis on the 'goodbye' to imply it was a farewell not a wishy-washy adieu.

Later on, as they sat in front of the crackling fire in Flora's own library she quizzed Nanny. 'There must be some way to implicate Mademoiselle oh-so-fluttery Jacqueline in the murder of Maud. I am sure she must have done it.'

Nanny eyed her. 'Unlikely. She probably wasn't even in the country at the time.'

Despondently, Flora ruffled her dog's head. 'I suppose you are right but it's a bit much having to compete for Busby's attention with a dachshund let alone a pert French miss.'

Dorothy gave Flora a pitiful look. *My dear, you think you compete with me for Busby's affection? Let's face it, there is* no *competition.*

# CHAPTER 13

## *A DOCTOR'S DILEMMA*

Dr Honour had had a trying morning and was pleased to be nearly home. He saw a figure walking slowly in front of him. He focused.

Yes, it was definitely Nurse Smythson ahead of him in the flurries of snow. A smile played around his lips; inexplicably he had felt a wave of… Of what? Joy was too strong a word, as was happiness. For a moment the emotion that the sight of her evoked escaped him, then he realised. It was peace. She was an oasis of tranquillity.

'Nurse Smythson,' he called. She carried on walking, perhaps even increasing her pace.

'Nurse Smythson!' he called again, quickening his own pace. He overtook her and faced her, just as they reached his home.

He blinked and stared as he gazed at her handsome features. With a jolt he realised she had been crying; her eyes were red-rimmed and her cheeks flushed. She tried to turn away from him, to hide her face. Instinctively, he put a hand out, just as a pitiful tear fell from her cheek. For a second, he glanced at the impression it made on his glove and felt his heart crush with sadness. Very gently, he put his arm around her. 'Come in; you're cold.'

To both of their surprise, she went with him into the warmth of his house and the sanctuary of his study. He called to the maid to bring them hot cocoa and then helped Nurse Smythson to take her old worn coat off.

She seemed a little dazed. He didn't say anything, just led her to the chair closest to the fire before putting another log on the blaze.

The cocoa arrived and with each sip Nurse Smythson felt more like herself. She risked peering up at the doctor from under her long dark lashes. Through her tear-soaked eyes, she realised that for days now she had hardly noticed the scarring down the left side of his face. Familiarity had taken the horror of it away and all she saw was his fine, chiselled features. Their eyes met.

'I'm sorry.' She blushed, embarrassed.

The kindness in his eyes was almost unbearable. 'What for? Having emotions? Am I right that this is about the time of year you lost your father?'

She nodded. 'But I'm being foolish – it was years ago.'

'Grief doesn't obey neat timetables,' he said quietly.

She began to say something, but her words were silenced by an angry intrusion.

His mother stood in the doorway, tall and thin, glowering at them. 'Victor!' Mrs Honour's voice was frosty. 'Lady Clarke will be here in a moment. I suggest you ask Nurse Smythson to leave.'

Dr Honour's body tensed; automatically his jaw clenched. He rose to his feet, feeling foolish at Nurse Smythson witnessing him being spoken to as if he was a naughty schoolboy. 'I will do no such thing. Nurse Smythson is my guest.'

Mrs Honour showed no emotion; she simply regarded the couple with a quiet contempt before slowly and with great deliberation announcing, 'I had hoped it wouldn't come to this, but I can see that you are determined to leave me no alternative.' She took in a breath, before continuing, 'As Nurse Smythson is aware, I have evidence that she had a strong motive for killing Maud.'

Dr Honour gasped, 'Mother!'

Nurse Smythson put her hand out and touched his clenched fist. 'No, let her finish. I would like you to know the truth.'

Mrs Honour looked down her nose at the young woman. With ice-grey eyes and a sneer on her face, she said, 'Nurse Smythson's father was involved in a shameful scandal.'

Flooded with disgust for his mother, Dr Honour unclenched his fist and wrapped his hand around Nurse Smythson's. He gave it a small squeeze as he said, 'If you are referring to her father taking his own life and the allegations of him manufacturing faulty equipment to the men at the front, then I already know and it in no way touches the esteem in which I hold Nurse Smythson.'

He glanced at the nurse; their eyes met.

His mother noted the interaction with displeasure and her lips tightened to a hard line. 'But did you also know that her father's business partner, the man who left him destitute and to carry all the shame, was none other than Maud's father?' An unpleasant smile crossed her face. 'I imagine the police would think that was an excellent motive for a murder. Even if they don't believe she is guilty, once I have finished spreading the word, the court of public opinion will condemn her.'

Nurse Smythson scrambled to her feet and grabbed her coat. 'I think I had better go.'

'Please stay.' Dr Honour's voice was weak. He knew his words were pointless; she was already through the door. He hesitated, unsure if it was better for Nurse Smythson to go or if he should stop her, but heard the front door open and firmly shut. Whatever he should have done, she was now gone while his mother remained.

His heart was pounding; his body was tense with impotent rage. He glowered at his mother. 'I will not tolerate your malicious attempts at blackmail.'

She regarded him coolly. 'And I will not tolerate you throwing away all the advantages that I sacrificed so much to give you. Nurse Smythson *will* leave the area, and you *will* marry Lady Clarke.' A half-smile played around her lips as she continued, 'Nurse Smythson's fate is in your hands; either she can go quietly – you can even write her a glowing reference – or,' here she fixed him with a glacial stare, 'I can let it be known that she murdered Maud.' With calm dignity, Mrs Honour swept from the room. Dr Honour's mind was in a turmoil but somewhere in the chaos his mind whispered, *How does she know so much about Nurse Smythson's father? Am I imagining it or did my father have business dealings with a Smythson?*

Standing in front of the mirror, which hung above the fireplace, he tried to gather his thoughts. Scattered images of Nurse Smythson, vulnerable and beautiful, swam in front of his mind's eye. He looked at his reflection and wondered who this stranger was that looked back at him. *Who is this pitiful man, who allows his mother to bully the woman he loves?*

He slammed his fist into the mirror. The crash of shattering glass gave him momentary relief, then the throb of pain engulfed him.

'Oh dear, I'm afraid that is going to hurt,' commented Lady Clarke, her voice calm and cultured. Dr Honour looked up to see her standing in the same doorway where his mother had been moments before.

Running footsteps heralded the arrival of the maid. Coolly, Lady Clarke took command. 'Please fetch some ice. The doctor has had an accident, he slipped and banged into the mirror but everything is quite alright now. He just needs a towel and little ice for his hand and perhaps something to wash it with, too.'

The girl bobbed a curtsey and scurried off while Dr Honour sunk wearily into the chair that was so recently vacated by Nurse Smythson. He was unconcerned by the shards of glass.

He eyed Lady Clarke. She was as composed and pretty as ever. There was not a curl out of place or even the smallest wrinkle in her dress.

'You heard?' he queried.

'Every word.' Her face was serious. After a pause she said, 'You know your mother means it; she will ruin the girl.'

He broke eye contact with her. Despair engulfed him.

'But you can save her.' He looked up at her, confused. She seemed totally calm. 'You could marry me.'

He started, but her expression gave nothing away about her emotions. Slowly he asked, 'What's in it for you?'

Now she smiled. 'Freedom,' was her simple response. He must have looked confused or surprised as she continued, 'You are not the usual sort of man who is paraded in front of me for matrimony.' She regarded him as if considering buying a new hat or a pound of potatoes. 'I feel a certain – fondness – for you. In time you may well develop tenderness, but I know you will always be courteous to me in our marriage.'

He raised an eyebrow. 'Courtesy? Is that all you want from a marriage?'

She gave a light laugh, 'For a doctor you are somewhat naïve. For a woman, courtesy in a marriage is a rarity. In comparison to the other suitors my parents have forced on me, you are quite a catch.' She paused before adding, in a voice barely above a whisper, 'And, in case you haven't noticed, virtually all the young men of your generation were killed in the war. There really is very little choice when it comes to eligible young men.'

# CHAPTER 14

### *FESTIVE FOLIAGE*

Flora was only slightly concerned by the size of the saw Tony had secured from Mr Bert. Debo had also borrowed a pair of clippers, a wheelbarrow and some sacking, all ideal for collecting festive foliage.

Busby surveyed the team. 'No Lavinia, Aunt Gigi or beautiful boys to help us?'

Debo beamed. 'Aunt Gigi said,' here she mimicked Gigi's voice and mannerisms to perfection, 'the only flora that interests me are lavish bouquets from an ardent lover.'

Busby grinned. 'Fair enough.'

Flora added, 'And Lavinia still seems to be in her good works era and has gone to visit Derek Adams.'

'Lucky him!' commented Tony wistfully. 'Although why Aunt Gigi sent Pierre and Anton with Lavinia as sort of sheepdogs, I can't imagine.'

The walk to the woods was short and pleasant, the sun even came out for part of it. The gentle hills and stone walls added to the picturesque setting. The leafless branches of trees rustled in the breeze and some crows cawed in the background.

As they approached the woods Debo and Tony lost no time in plunging into its depths while Busby and Flora chose to skirt the outer perimeter.

'Gosh! Look at that mistletoe!' exclaimed Flora, her eyes sparkling as she pointed at a round mass of green leaves with many small pearl-like berries nestling high up in the bare branches of a lime tree. The tree was growing out from a thick hedge and towered over a gate.

Busby glanced at it. 'Yes, but without a ladder it will be impossible to reach.'

Flora flashed him what could only be described as a saucy look, before declaring, 'Want to bet?' She headed over to the gate and despite the limitations of her skirt and heavy boots, she climbed on top of it with ease.

'Be careful!' laughed Busby. His eyes were fixed on her, his mind battling between concern, amusement and admiration.

'Nothing to it!' called Flora, her cheeks pink with exertion and excitement. From the height of the gate, it was easy enough to reach the lower branches of the tree. She almost lost her footing but steadied herself. She continued her ascent. 'I've always been an excellent tree climber,' she explained through her puffs of breath. Each exhalation made a little cloud in the frosty air. Halfway up she paused to look around. 'Fabulous view from up here; I can see the church and, oh, Farrington Hall looks so pretty.' She swayed precariously as she looked out.

'Can we please stay focused on the task in hand?' enquired Busby.

Flora grinned. 'Right oh!'

She soon reached the mistletoe. Carefully gripping a nearby branch with one hand, she took out her pocket-knife with her other hand. It was the work of a moment to cut the mistletoe free.

'Here! Catch!' she called down to Busby as she tossed her prize towards him.

He caught it with ease, and she began her descent.

It was only then she remembered that going down was harder than going up. *Oh!* She glanced around, fighting down the butterflies in her tummy. *How on earth did I get up here? Oh help! I haven't any idea which branches I used as holds on my way up.*

'Are you alright?' enquired Busby, sensing her dithering.

'Oh yes, fine!' she lied, trying to swallow her rising panic.

*Get a hold of yourself, Flora!* she told herself sternly. Carefully, she grabbed one sturdy branch while lowering her foot down to tentatively feel for a safe purchase. With relief, she found a secure spot for her right foot and then her left.

She managed to get most of the way down before disaster hit. Just as she was levering her weight onto her left foot there was an alarming cracking sound. Flora froze. Her heart raced.

Busby heard it too. He drew in his breath.

After a moment when nothing happened Flora began to breathe more easily. She grasped a nearby damp branch. She wobbled and to her dismay felt the security of the branch slipping through her fingers while at the same time the branch she was standing on let out another crack and fell away.

She felt herself falling, as if in slow motion. She had the fleeting thought, *This is going to hurt.* She landed with a whoosh, not on the expected hard ground but on Busby.

For a moment they lay quite still; Busby because he was winded and because Flora was on top of him, while Flora chose not to move because she was enjoying the situation. *It's been a long time since I've been this close to a man*

It was she who, with great reluctance, opened her eyes first. A moment later Busby's eyes opened. For a few blissful seconds, they looked at each other. His hazel eyes were shining and softened as he lost himself in hers. Flora felt as if she was floating. Warmth filled her body, and she was dizzy with happiness. *It's as if we are lost in a time and space known only to each other,* she thought, recalling a line from one of Nanny's more lurid romances.

Flora was not sure if it was the nearby cawing of a crow or the sound of a twig snapping but in an instant, the spell broke. Both Busby and Flora suddenly recalled who they were and where they were and most importantly, what was appropriate behaviour between and police officer and a wealthy widow.

They sprang apart and struggled to their feet.

'Are you alright?' enquired Busby.

'Oh yes, rather!' she said brightly while privately wondering, *Is it possible that I may have an undiagnosed heart problem? The old ticker seems to be racing.* As an outlet for her emotions, she started vigorously brushing twigs and leaves from her tweed coat. She was very aware that he was watching her rather too intently for her peace of mind.

He took a step towards her. 'You've missed a bit.'

*Can he be coming down with something? His voice seems a bit husky. Come to think of it, my throat feels a bit tight.*

She risked a glance at him then wished she hadn't as her heartbeat became even more erratic. *Gosh! He's awfully close.*

She tried to swallow. 'What?' She realised that the word had come out as a sigh.

'Here,' he murmured, stepping so close that shat she could feel his warm breath on her face.

'What?' she asked again, wondering why, with all the money her parents had spent on her education, she couldn't think of anything more eloquent to say. *It really is most unsettling to have him looking at me like this.* She swallowed. *And I don't think he could be any nearer.*

'You have a twig in your hair.'

She blinked up at him. 'Really?' She automatically raised a hand to her head. She caught her breath as, very firmly but gently, he took her hand in his.

His eyes were fixed on her as he murmured, 'Let me.'

With a jolt, she felt his fingers brush against her cheek. Somewhere, along the way, he had shed his gloves, and the touch of his skin on hers sent a pleasurable shiver through her body. Without thinking, she edged closer to him as he carefully plucked the twig from one of curls that had escaped from the confines of her hat.

His eyes were locked on hers. *Why have I never noticed those fiery amber flecks before? Or how large his pupils are? Positively swimmy!* Blushing, with her heart pounding as she struggled for breath, she thought, *Oh golly!*

To her dismay she heard herself blurt out, 'Gosh! Thanks awfully!'

She wasn't sure if it made things better or worse when he grinned and chuckled, 'Think nothing of it.'

*Get a grip Flora! You are meant to be a woman of the world,* she chastened herself. *Come on, it's not as if you're a blushing virgin – you were married, for goodness's sake.* The thought didn't help as a very small voice, in the recesses of her mind reminded her, *But that was a jolly long time ago.*

She gazed up at him. *Why have I never noticed how delightful his neck and throat are or the dimple on his chin? Can an Adam's apple be called attractive? Perhaps I have never observed it before because I have never looked at him from this angle before.*

Tilting her chin up, she breathed out a quiet, 'Your scarf has gone awry.'

He seemed to be having difficulty speaking, but managed to get out a stilted, 'It has?'

She nodded. 'Let me fix it for you.'

Tentatively she raised her hands, the action was as if she was about to encircle his neck.

'What-ho, Mummy! Talk about slackers! Is that miserly bit of mistletoe all you two have managed to collect? Just look at the heaps of holly and ivy Tony and I have gathered!'

# CHAPTER 15

*FLORA HAS A TRYING TIME WITH MRS SCRUBS AND MADEMOISELLE JACQUELINE*

Flora decided that she really must go to the post office in the village and post the few Christmas cards she had managed to write. Right up until the moment she took the Morgan out of her garage, she had been vacillating between it being far too late to post them and it was her duty to at least try. She was also feeling slightly guilty that Lavinia had been so good about visiting poor, brave Derek Adams when she herself hadn't bothered. As the Adams' house was near to the village post office, she decided to kill two birds with one stone and visit Derek after posting the cards.

She was surprised and delighted as she drove up to the house to see Busby just in front of her. They parked their cars side by side and smiled at each other a little more than was necessary.

Now was her chance to impress him with her demure poise; unfortunately, all she could think to say was, 'What-ho!'

Amused, he raised an eyebrow and smiled in such a way that the laughter lines around his eyes creased. She noticed that his freckles were less pronounced in the winter than in the summer but the cleft in his chin was just as adorable as ever.

She thought she might be able to save the situation by injecting a bit of sophisticated conversation, but instead she blurted out, 'I was just passing. Well, I needed to send off dratted Christmas cards.'

'Bit late, isn't it?' he enquired with a grin that made Flora's knees go weak.

She heard herself gushing, 'Rather, should have gone weeks

ago. I always have such good intentions but—' She shrugged her shoulders, then felt rather flustered by the warmth and intensity of his gaze.

'But why are you here rather than at the post office?'

His voice was deep, and Flora found herself thinking, *Am I going quite gaga? I want to describe his voice as dreamy.*

She blinked and blurted out, 'Guilt!'

Teasingly, he enquired, 'Do you want to confess to murdering Maud?'

'No, but I just feel guilty that I haven't called on Mr Adams more.'

'As the lady of the manor?'

She wasn't sure if he was laughing at her. Suddenly she realised she didn't mind if he was. 'As a neighbour,' she said, mustering a bit of dignity. Regaining a sense of reason through all her giddiness she gave him a shrewd look. 'What about you? Why are you here? Do you have new evidence?'

Busby shook his head. 'Nothing so exciting. Mr Adams telephoned and asked me to call; he didn't say why.'

They reached the house and Busby knocked. To Flora's surprise it was opened by Derek Adams himself rather than by Mrs Scrubs or even Nurse Smythson.

Once again, there were dark circles around his sunken eyes, suggesting a sleepless night. His grey, well-oiled hair was dishevelled, and Flora soon saw why; every second moment he ran an agitated hand through his locks. She wondered what had happened for him to have had such an emotional setback.

He wore baggy trousers, which were the fashion among the young men of the day but which looked odd on a middle-aged man. He also sported a garishly-bright sweater and matching tie, which might have passed on a golf course but certainly was odd for an afternoon at home. Flora averted her eyes. *I can't bring myself to look at his shoes – I suspect they are two-toned.*

'Come in, come in.' He ushered them into the drawing room which held its habitual dismal fire. 'So wise of you, Inspector, to think of bringing Mrs Farrington – a woman's touch and comfort.

Such a good idea to have a lady present if we have to confront her.'

Flora would have liked to enquire who 'her' was but there wasn't an opportunity.

'I—' began Busby

Derek Adams ignored this. He was in full flow. 'Do sit down,' he urged, 'It's all most distressing, most distressing.' Busby and Flora obliged but while they sat, he strode up and down the room wringing his hands. 'I do so hate to think ill of anyone but facts are facts, however distasteful.'

Busby and Flora exchanged a puzzled look, before Busby took command. 'Mr Adams, would you kindly tell us what this is all about?'

Derek Adams stopped pacing and stared at him, his eyes large and his mouth slack.

At this moment there was a slight clutter of china and Mrs Scrubs entered the room, looking every inch like a tortoise. Derek went very still and strangely silent.

Without a smile she stated, 'I saw you had company, so I took the liberty of bringing in the tea tray.'

She put it down none too gently on the side table and left.

Even after her departure, Derek remained in his trance-like state.

Flora looked at him. *At this rate, that tea will remain in the pot, and I won't ever get a sip of it.*

Without waiting for a reply, she stood up and sorted out the cups and the tea. The tea set was a similar sleek modern design to her own favourite one but whereas hers was a mass of jazz colours this was an insipid white. Flora gave Maud a fleeting thought. *She probably chose it because she thought it was chic rather than just boring.*

A few moments later Flora looked directly at Derek Adams. 'Now we all have tea, why don't you sit down and explain to us what has distressed you. Have you had a phone call? A letter? A conversation?'

Still pale, he confirmed, 'A letter – of sorts.'

'Very good.' Flora smiled and, in a voice more appropriate to speaking to a young child than a middle-aged widower continued, 'Have a sip of your tea and tell us all about it.' She had put extra sugar in Derek's cup in the hope it would boost his faculties and clarify his thoughts.

Obediently, he sipped and appeared to like the taste as he took another mouthful before addressing Flora and Busby. 'I found this in the pocket one of Maud's dresses.' He held out a crumpled piece of paper. Busby took it and while he looked at it, Derek continued. 'It's a letter Maud wrote to Mrs Scrubs – well, a draft of a letter. It says that Maud had suspected that Mrs Scrubs had not been honest about her past and that she had paid a private investigator to look into it.' Here a misplaced sense of pride in his late wife suffused his expression with a hint of warmth. 'She was frightfully on the ball with that sort of thing.'

Flora leaned forward. 'So what had the investigator discovered?'

Derek stared at his hands, evidently embarrassed, his tone barely above a whisper. 'That Mrs Scrubs isn't a married widow, that she's never been married, that she faked her references and that she was born out of wedlock.'

Busby, who was reading the letter, nodded. 'Mrs Adams does rather labour the point of Mrs Scrubs being illegitimate.'

Derek Adams looked up. 'Maud took a very strong line on that sort of thing. That's why she goes on to say that she is not only giving Mrs Scrubs her notice but is also reporting her to the police about the forged references. I am very much afraid that we now know who murdered Maud and why.'

As if on cue, Mrs Scrubs walked in, armed with a coal bucket. 'Excuse me, I saw the fire was low when I brought the tea in.'

She froze, aware that all eyes were upon her and that Busby was on his feet. She dropped the coal bucket and gaped at Busby, then Flora and finally at her employer who flushed and hastily looked away.

Busby ushered her in. 'I think you had better read this.'

He gave her the letter and as she read her hands started to tremble and the colour drained from her face. She swayed.

Flora leapt to her feet. 'Here Mrs Scrubs, do sit down.' With a comforting hand on the woman's bony elbow, she urged her to the nearest chair.

For a moment she sat with her head in her hands. When she looked up, her eyes were red. She glanced around at each of them and with a whine in her voice declared, 'It's simply not true. I wouldn't lie to you.'

*And therein lies the problem,* thought Flora. *We all know you lie constantly.*

'Did you receive a letter like this from Mrs Adams before she died?' asked Busby calmly.

'No!' she shrieked. Her response was too vehement, and Flora knew without a doubt that she was lying.

'We need to go over your previous statement,' said Busby. 'Perhaps you would accompany me down to the station.'

She nodded and stood up. Her eyes were still red-rimmed with brimming tears but with her shoulders back and her chin held high, she said with great dignity, 'Excuse me while I get my hat and coat.'

After she left, there was an awkward silence in the room broken only by the crackle and hiss of the dwindling fire. Flora jumped as the quiet was interrupted by heavy banging on the front door.

Derek looked up. 'Who on earth can that be?' He was a shade of pale green and evidently not up to dealing with unexpected visitors.

'I'll see,' announced Flora, leaping to her feet.

'I should go and see to Mrs Scrubs,' said Busby, also rising.

Flora opened the door to a happy, chattering and – to her mind – most unwelcome group.

There on the doorstep, were a jovial Colonel and Mrs Ford, their two immaculately-dressed daughters, both of whom, judging by their red noses, had colds, and an annoyingly beautiful Mademoiselle Jacqueline.

Flora's eyes swept over both parents and offspring and rested on Mademoiselle Jacqueline. *How can anyone look so fresh faced and brimming with health in December? It's positively indecent.*

Colonel Ford boomed, 'Mrs Farrington, please forgive the intrusion but we felt so bad that we hadn't called on poor old Mr Adams.'

Mrs Ford moved into the hallway nodding vigorously. 'Quite, quite, but it could not be helped; we have had so many obligations.'

Colonel Ford guffawed with laughter, his ample belly shaking with mirth and his face turning the colour of aged port. 'What she means is we have lots of aged visitors who expect a Christmas visit, which is why we have the girls with us. We're just passing after seeing Aunt Phillipa in Bournemouth.'

Mrs Ford interjected, 'But not to worry, they'll be no trouble. Mademoiselle Jacqueline is simply wonderful.'

They all looked at Mademoiselle Jacqueline who managed to look both beautiful and modest. She looked down, fluttering her eyelashes becomingly.

'I bet she is,' said Flora sourly and then realised that Busby was just behind her and had heard every word.

Drawn by the chatter, Derek had also joined them in the hall. 'Tea?' he asked. He still had an unhealthy pallor and hollow eyes, despite all the sugar Flora had put in his tea.

Flora was extremely relieved when they declined. *I am pretty certain Mrs Scrubs won't be offering to make us all tea, having just been accused of murder.*

The Colonel's voice boomed once more. 'I can see you are not quite the ticket so we won't stop. Just wanted to give you our regards.'

'I'll walk you to your car,' said Derek, putting his shoulders back with an effort and striding forward.

Flora was delighted to see them leave but less thrilled at finding herself in close proximity to Busby and Jacqueline.

The Frenchwoman rested an elegant hand on Busby's arm. Pouting with rosebud lips and gazing up adoringly at his with large cornflower-blue eyes, she murmured, 'Oh Claudius, I am so looking forward to dancing with you at the Lords and Ladies Ball.'

Busby seemed unable to speak and was looking rather flushed.

*Well really!* thought Flora. She firmly removed Jacqueline's hand and said crisply, 'I'm sure you are but I believe Mrs Ford is beckoning you. Best be on your way – so sad you can't stay and chat to Claudius.' She propelled Mademoiselle Jacqueline towards the door.

The young woman bestowed on Flora a radiant smile. 'Did you know Mrs Farrington, Claudius dances divinely.'

'Yes, yes dear, I'm sure he's quite heavenly.' Flora more or less pushed her out of the door. 'Goodbye,' she said crisply as she firmly shut the door. Turning around she coldly regarded Busby.

'Umm,' he stammered.

'Yes, well, I think you had better go and find Mrs Scrubs.'

# CHAPTER 16

## A BIT OF PRE-BALL BEAUTY PREPARATION

While Flora had been dealing with Mrs Scrubs and Mademoiselle Jacqueline, her great aunt and her daughter had been having a relaxing time. Gigi and Debo were lying side by side on Gigi's lavish four-poster bed. Debo was in her normal clothes with her shoes kicked off while Gigi was wrapped in a magnificent silk kimono. Their faces were white with a luxuriant face cream that Gigi had had specially made. She swore it was the only thing a girl needed for perfect skin. Over their eyes they had cooling cotton wool pads, again steeped in a secret tonic, known only to Gigi and her dermatologist.

The room was scented by lilies. Gigi explained that the vast bouquet that had arrived earlier was from an admirer.

'Goodness, Gigi, what are the chances that you not only grew up in a children's home but the very one we broke down outside!' exclaimed Debo.

'Life is often like that. I was Mrs Pie's first girl,' answered Gigi complacently. 'Real life has more coincidences than you would believe if you read them in a book.'

Debo was less interested in the role of coincidences in life than in Aunt Gigi's history. 'Was it frightful, growing up in a home?'

'Not really. You see, I wasn't so very young when my parents died. I was about your age.'

'Mummy still thinks I'm a baby,' sighed Debo.

Gigi gave a sympathetic laugh. 'Lots of people are earning their own living at your age.'

'I suppose my ideas about orphanages are all from Dickens – Oliver Twist and gruel.'

'Money is a problem with most charitable homes.'

'I guess it takes a lot of raffles and jumble sales to run a home like Mrs Pie's.'

'Well, wealthy individuals, like me, give donations and then there are always legacies left in wills.' There was a silent pause then Gigi said, 'I have a question for you – it's along the lines of learning to make a decision when there is no good decision.'

'Is making tricky decisions high on your list of necessary life skills? Like Nanny believes that learning resilience is vital – she sees self-pity as the death of life.'

Gigi snorted. 'She does have a point.'

There was another pause before Debo prompted her, 'So what is your moral question?'

'Without money, Mrs Pie cannot take in children. She knows that if a child cannot come to her, they may end up on the streets.'

'So, money is of the utmost importance to Mrs Pie.'

'Yes, now, if you were Mrs Pie, would you accept money from a bad person or an illegal source?'

'How bad?' asked Debo, her voice laced with excitement.

'About as bad as it could be.'

Flora wandered in and interrupted their conversation. 'You meanies, you might have told me you were having a beauty session. Budge up, there's room for three on this grand old bed. Those Georgians certainly knew a thing or two about bed-building.' She scrambled up on to the vast four-poster bed.

'Do you want some wonder cream to pop on your face?' asked Debo. 'It's on the side table.'

'No, thank you, I don't feel strong enough to deal with the mess.' She leant back on the pillow with a deep sigh.

'Trying day?' enquired Gigi.

'Rather,' sighed Flora again.

'Do tell,' exclaimed Debo.

'I popped into the village to post some Christmas cards and—'

'Bit late isn't it?' interrupted Gigi.

'Yes,' agreed Flora a little tightly. 'Well, I thought I would take advantage of being in that region to call in on Derek Adams.'

Aunt Gigi chuckled. 'I take it you didn't want Lavinia being the only saint in the family?'

'Exactly. I arrived to find Busby there.'

'Lucky you,' commented Aunt Gigi.

Flora ignored her. 'Mr Adams was in an awful state. He had found a letter, well the draft of a letter, from Maud to Mrs Scrubs.'

'Saying what?' asked Debo eagerly.

'If you will both stop interrupting me, I will tell you.' Flora wasn't finding this interlude as relaxing as she had hoped. She allowed a moment of silence before she continued, 'It raised her telling lies. Apparently, she also fabricated her references, and it also accused her of being illegitimate – as if that's a criminal offence.'

'Illegitimacy might not be a crime for the child, but it does explain why the woman lies – she will have grown up having to hide who she is,' said Gigi thoughtfully.

Debo was thrilled. 'Sounds like she is now Busby's top suspect – talk about having a motive.'

'Yes,' agreed Flora doubtfully.

'You don't sound very pleased, Mummy. Surely you are delighted that there is another suspect other than Paul Draycott?'

Flora sat up, reached for the pot of cream and began smearing it on her face, having changed her mind about the mess verses the beauty benefits. As she beautified herself, she explained, 'I'm not sure I am any happier about her being Maud's murderer than I am about Paul Draycott. Obviously if it was she who tried to kill you Debo, darling, I shouldn't be best pleased.'

'Glad to hear it,' said Debo dryly.

Again, Flora ignored the remark and continued, 'I think my lingering affection for Mrs Scrubs is her resemblance to my pet tortoise. I was very fond of that tortoise.'

'So, Mummy, if you don't want the murderer to be her or Paul Draycott, who do you want it to be?'

'Mademoiselle Jacqueline,' muttered Flora under her breath.

'I would be quite happy if she was carted off to His Majesty's Prison Holloway.'

'Sorry, Mummy, I didn't catch that?'

'Nothing, darling, I was just talking to myself. I am out of ideas.'

'Well, lots of the villagers reported seeing two beautiful angels on the morning of her death.'

'Well, that's difficult to prove.' Aunt Gigi chuckled. 'And angels are notoriously difficult to prosecute.'

Debo continued, 'My money is on Mrs Honour; she is a really unpleasant specimen, and I did see her acting suspiciously.'

'I totally agree that she is more than capable of murder – she frequently gives me looks that suggest she could happily kill me – but what would her motive be for murdering Maud?' queried Flora.

'Maud seems to have delighted in blackmailing anyone she could. Perhaps Mrs Honour has a dark secret beneath her starchy exterior,' Aunt Gigi suggested.

'Perhaps,' agreed Flora.

'Then there's Nurse Smythson. Don't forget, Mummy, you told me that when you arrived at Derek Adams' house, just after the body had been found, Dr Honour was berating Nurse Smythson over some missing morphine. I would say that makes her a sure-fire suspect for having drugged Mrs Adams and then drowning her.'

Flora would have replied but Aunt Gigi took command. 'Enough of this chatter. If the cream is to do its miraculous work, we all need to totally relax. Silence!'

# CHAPTER 17

### *THE BALL*

In the blink of an eye, the evening of the ball arrived.

'What could possibly go wrong, Mummy? Do stop fussing about the ball and help me to do up the back button on this dress.'

'What indeed?' murmured Flora. A long list of possible, if not highly likely, catastrophes loomed in Flora's mind. Instead of voicing them she changed topic. 'Now, let me look at you.'

Debo was wearing a neat dress in a dark green that suited her complexion.

Matter of factly, Debo explained, 'Nanny says I am neither fish nor fowl – she calls it that awkward age where one is no longer a child but not an adult yet. She reckons this dress is perfect; it clearly proclaims that I am out of the nursery but still chained to the schoolroom.' She caught her mother's eyes and they both giggled.

'Gosh,' laughed Flora, 'what a long-winded way to say that you look jolly nice.'

'So do you, Mummy,' said Debo as she admired Flora's deep-red dress which skimmed her body and showed off her trim figure and a daring amount of her ankles.

'Thank you, darling,' said Flora as she applied a touch more rouge and lipstick.

Debo regarded her own bare arms in the mirror. 'I'm a bit concerned I will get frightfully cold later on in the evening.'

Lavinia, who was draped in the armchair, looking impossibly beautiful in blue, said, 'If you do, feel free to go to my room and help yourself my stole, Debo. It will go perfectly with your dress.'

'Gosh, thanks awfully. Jolly decent of you.'

There was a knock on the door. Debo opened it and found it was Tony. He was frowning, his mop of black hair was dishevelled, and his top shirt-stud was undone. He held the black tie in his outstretched hand. 'I say, Mother, can you help me with this dratted thing?'

'Allow me,' said Lavinia who stood and walked slowly towards Tony. The boy turned crimson, swallowed and then appeared to stop breathing.

*Oh bless!* thought Flora as she brushed past her son. 'I'd better go and see how the preparations are going.'

Farrington Hall was certainly looking magnificent; holly and ivy adorned every possible banister and picture frame. Flora could hear the band tuning up. She wasn't sure if she enjoyed the pre-ball bustle or whether it was giving her a headache. She passed her maids, Mavis and Gladys, on the stairs. They were both in high spirits – giggling and exchanging whispers. Flora was honestly able to say how beautiful they both looked. This was met by more giggles and long explanations as to which films and movie stars the dresses were based on. Mavis was in a dark-green dress and Gladys in red. *They both look stunning. I bet Mrs Wilkes is having forty fits over the way both dresses show off a scandalous amount of the girls' backs.*

'We've lit the candles on the Christmas trees,' announced Mavis.

'And it looks grand,' added Gladys, her eyes sparkling with excitement.

Flora smiled. 'I look forward to seeing it.'

The tree was, indeed, magnificent. Tall and straight, it filled every room with its pine scent. Oranges, pricked by cloves and hung by red ribbons, added to the seasonal perfume. Endless glass baubles reflected the light of all the little candles which were burning on the tips of the boughs.

Flora surveyed the garlands and listened to the band. *It's going to be a wonderful evening.* She bit her lip as doubts and worries threatened to overcome her optimism.

Dorothy, who had been following Flora around the house and watching all the preparations with interest, looked up as her mistress said out loud, 'There are always so many last-minute details to attend to – and so many things that could go wrong.'

Dorothy cocked her head on one side. *Nothing can go wrong for me. I have my bone at the ready and Nanny has placed my basket in her room by the fire so that I can settle down for a quiet evening undisturbed by all this nonsense.* A wicked gleam came into her eye. *Of course, I may pop out and nip the odd guest on the ankle.*

Flora sought out Roberts. *He is always such a calming figure.* As expected, she found him in the reception area, arranging champagne flutes on trays. He looked very distinguished in white tie and tails, with his silver fox hair swept back.

He smiled at her approach. 'I have hidden the best champagne flutes as I anticipate all the glasses being broken by midnight.'

Flora laughed. 'What, by inebriated lords acting as footmen?'

'Precisely.'

'It's all a bit of a pretence, isn't it?'

He raised an eyebrow as he regarded her, 'What is?'

'This Lords and Ladies Ball.'

'How?'

'The whole idea that for this one evening those above stairs are meant to do all the work while the servants enjoy a rare bit of leisure. The sad reality is that all my industrious staff seems to be working harder than ever so that the local "great and the good" can play at being servants. Mrs Wilkes is quietly unravelling in the privacy of her kitchen.'

Roberts laughed and there was a distinct twinkle in his eye as he replied, 'It's always like that in this world. There are life's doers and life's…'

It was Flora's turn to raise a quizzical eyebrow. 'And the world's idlers?' she enquired. With a sigh she added, 'I fear I fall into the idlers' category.' Miserably, she lamented, 'Here we are, Christmas Eve and I have totally failed to get Paul Draycott home in time for Christmas. I keep thinking about how sad both Claire and Betty must be.'

Roberts popped a champagne cork and poured a glass for her. Handing it to her he said, 'To celebrate being on the brink of success.' He poured himself a glass and clinked it with Flora's, as he announced a toast. 'To your imminent victory.'

'Thank you,' acknowledged Flora.

They both took a refreshing sip.

Roberts smiled. 'This is quite like old times.'

'You're thinking of the ball in France?'

He nodded, then regarded Flora with a fatherly smile before remarking, 'If I may say so, you look quite delightful.'

Flora smiled and smoothed her wine-red dress. She was glad he approved, despite the daring amount of ankle and back the dress revealed.

'You may indeed. Thank you.'

'This is quite like old times; you wore a red dress at the ball at the chateau.'

Flora laughed. 'Well, I hope no one tries to murder me this evening.'

Roberts smiled. 'Who knows, the night is still young.'

Debo ran down the stairs and joined her mother. 'It all looks simply splendid, doesn't it, Mummy?'

Flora glanced around and had to agree.

Nanny lumbered up to them. To Debo's disgust she had made no change to her usual sombre black attire.

'Nanny!' she exclaimed. 'You could have at least made a bit of an effort.'

Nanny grunted. 'Personally I don't see the need.'

Flora and Debo exchanged a glance, and, with the aplomb of a magician pulling a white rabbit from out of a top hat, Flora displayed the family diamond tiara she had been hiding behind her back.

'Here you go,' declared Flora as Debo placed it on Nanny's head. 'This will add a bit of a sparkle to your costume. We knew you wouldn't dress up so we took the liberty of liberating the family tiara from the safe.'

Nanny grunted again and surveyed herself in a nearby mirror. It was half lost amid her mass of grey curls but nonetheless added a touch of grandeur to her otherwise sombre dress.

Not surprisingly, Mrs Honour was already at the hall. She coldly watched the tiara incident, then turned her most gushing smile on Lady Clarke as she walked through the front door.

'You look quite beautiful, my dear.' She beamed as Lady Clarke shrugged off her fur. 'Perkins, take Lady Clarke's fur to the cloakroom and mind you don't harm it!' she commanded a small boy in shorts. Reluctantly he stopped playing marbles and obliged.

Looking around at those assembled in the hall, Lady Clarke explained to Flora, 'What fun this is! I wanted to dress up in a cap and apron, but dear Amanda said that that was not the thing, so here I am.' She held out her arms to show off her exquisite mink fur stole and an obscene number of diamonds on her gloved wrist.

Flora blinked at the notion anyone calling the stern and starchy Mrs Honour 'dear Amanda'.

Lavinia was walking past with a tray of canapés and Mrs Honour lost no time in issuing her next command. 'Lavinia, be an angel and show Lady Clarke what to do. I need to stay by the door to greet the guests.'

Lavinia stiffened but obliged.

Flora was slightly perturbed at hearing Mrs Honour declare that she would be greeting the guests at the door. *Surely, I am the hostess? Shouldn't I be the one to do that? Oh goodness, what should I do? If only I was one of those forthright battle-axes, I would simply fix Mrs Honour with a steely stare and crisply inform her that there is absolutely no need for her to be anywhere near the front door. Perhaps I would even follow it up by suggesting her skills would be better employed doing some menial tasks in the scullery.* She sighed, knowing such boldness was quite beyond her.

In the end she settled for hovering beside Mrs Honour and trying to nip in to greet new arrivals before the other lady could. It was both unsatisfactory and undignified, but it was the best she could manage.

Dr Honour arrived. He shook Flora's hand. 'I'm sorry I wasn't here earlier to help; I needed to attend to a difficult birth.'

Flora smiled. 'Clearly, you have already fulfilled your village duties for the day, so I officially excuse you from serving duty.'

He wasn't really listening to her, rather he was scanning the rooms beyond her.

Mrs Honour noticed his distraction and with just a hint of satisfaction said, 'Lady Clarke went that way with Lavinia.'

He didn't pay attention to his mother any more than he had Flora; instead, he turned to look at the new arrivals. To his obvious pleasure, his eyes alighted on Nurse Smythson who had just entered the house on Mr Adams' arm.

His eyes grew large, and it occurred to Flora that it was the first time she'd seen the doctor smile.

She managed to greet Mr Adams before Mrs Honour got to him. 'How kind of you to come especially…' She paused, realising that she could hardly say, "especially as you are probably quite aware that I suspect your wife was murdered and my daughter was looking for clues in your house." Instead, she finished with a neutral, 'In the circumstances.'

Flora regarded his greying temples and his rather flamboyant tie. *That's definitely not mourning attire.* He murmured something about, 'Just doing my bit,' before hurrying off in search of champagne. As she watched him go, she mused, *He does carry off the air of saintly martyrdom while still enjoying his pleasures rather well. No wonder Lavinia has decided that he is a person upon whom she can lavish her good works.*

Dr Honour further earned Flora's admiration by totally ignoring his mother's disapproving stares while he helped Nurse Smythson off with her coat and commented on how lovely her dress was. It was a most becoming shade of blue and showed off her figure to perfection. To Flora's eyes it was desperately dated, but what did that matter when Dr Honour was so obviously enchanted?

Flora soon had her own distractions as Busby was waiting to be greeted. He looked quite dashing in his evening attire and

Flora's mind momentarily strayed to the bunch of mistletoe they had collected together and that now hung in a secluded alcove. *I must remember to show it to him before the evening is over.* When he saw her, he smiled and she felt her tummy flip in a rather girlish way. Her mind raced. *Just how many dances can I enjoy with him and still retain a shred of my reputation?*

To her dismay, before she could give him the warmest of welcomes, Jacqueline arrived, looking infuriatingly beautiful.

The young Frenchwoman latched onto his arm and fluttered her excessively long eyelashes at him. *Why did I shut Dorothy away? I need her – she would never let Jacqueline be that familiar with Busby. Sometimes a girl just needs to bite an ankle.*

Flora thought she detected an apology in Busby's eyes as Mademoiselle Jacqueline whisked him past her with an expertise that belied her youth.

Mrs Ford and her husband, Colonel Ford accompanied by their daughters, had shared a car with their governess and arrived at the door moments later. Colonel Ford was as portly and jovial as ever. Flora noted that Mrs Ford, in her evening splendour, displayed traces of the prettiness of her youth. Unfortunately, Mrs Ford did not hurry past Flora with the same haste that Mademoiselle Jacqueline had shown; on the contrary she seemed keen to confide in her.

'Don't they make a lovely couple?' she declared gazing over at the beautiful governess and Busby. The couple were heading towards the dance floor.

Flora looked at how well matched they were in height and looks, not to mention youth. Feeling rather sick, she agreed.

'We'll be devastated to lose her, won't we dear?' She looked to her husband who grunted. Then with a beam she added, 'But who are we to stand in the way of true love?'

Flora wondered whether, as the hostess, she could simply leave the party, perhaps head off to the Ritz in London or better still Paris. *Actually, anywhere would be better than staying here, watching Busby and Jacqueline.*

Gigi had waited until she was certain most of the guests would have arrived before making her grand entrance. She had primed the band and upon a signal they played a fanfare. As had been Gigi's intention, all eyes swivelled to look up at her.

She was quite a sight to behold. Her dress was a truly magnificent pink creation, which shimmered; hundreds of tiny crystals reflected and twinkled under the light. Her hair had been coiffed to perfection and was adorned with a pink ostrich feather. She was flanked by the beautiful boys who looked more breathtaking than ever in their white tie. Each sported a pink rosebud in their buttonhole in honour of Gigi.

Majestically she slowly sailed down the staircase with a beautiful boy on each arm.

Mrs Honour looked horrified. Flora was delighted.

Debo let out a sigh of admiration. 'Now that's what I call an entrance! Can I do it next year, Mummy?'

Flora, with a wistful smile, murmured, 'Perhaps not next year but certainly when you are older. I must say, I rather fancy it myself.'

In the short time since their arrival, Dr Honour and Nurse Smythson had made a surprising discovery. They had delighted in dancing in each other's arms. Never had Dr Honour danced so lightly. Nurse Smythson, for her part, felt a glorious surge of happiness as she looked him in the eyes and allowed him to whirl her around the room. Eventually, breathless and giddy from both the dancing and their growing attraction, they peeled off into the quieter library where a fire burned and there was a handy tray of drinks.

Dr Honour could not stop gazing at Nurse Honour; it was as if he was unable to believe that there could be anyone in the world as wonderful as she was. Even more surprisingly, she was looking at him in exactly the same way. He poured them both a much-needed drink.

It was after about the third reviving sip that Nurse Smythson's gaze wandered from Dr Honour's eyes to the bunch of mistletoe. A mischievous glint came into her eyes. He followed the line of her sight and as he saw the mistletoe he gave out a low, happy chuckle. He took her by the hand and led her over to stand under the mistletoe. He paused, aware that both of their hearts were beating fast and that the tension between them was electric.

He gently pulled her towards him and their lips brushed with such tenderness that a tear trickled down her cheek. The next kiss was longer, imbued with passion. For an eternity they were lost in each other.

When eventually they paused, they stood with their arms wrapped around each other, both surprised and at the same time knowing that they were meant to be together. They looked at each other and laughed, then the mood turned more serious as they leaned in for another kiss. Their lips had barely touched when they were interrupted by a small boy with grubby knees and a runny nose.

''Scuse me, Doctor, but I has a message for you.'

The doctor and Nurse Smythson quickly disengaged. Dr Honour laughed as he said, 'Thank you, Perkins.'

The small boy handed it over and ran off, no doubt keen to join his friends.

Dr Honour took the note, read it and sighed. 'I'm going to have to go. One of my elderly patients is in pain. He hasn't got long for this world and—'

Nurse Smythson nodded. 'Of course, you must go and do all you can for him. Shall I go with you?' There was a hopeful note in her voice as she looked steadily at him.

With reluctance he shook his head. 'Better not. If the end is nigh, I suspect his daughter would prefer not to have a stranger present.'

Nurse Smythson nodded again, then gave him a light peck on his cheek. 'I'll see you later.'

Euphoric, he walked away, leaving her with her thoughts. She toyed with the flower he had placed in her hair and felt herself blushing. For the first time since her father had died she felt a sense of safety, of belonging.

Her happy musings were abruptly interrupted by Mrs Honour's sharp voice. 'I see that my son received the message I sent.'

Nurse Smythson spun around to look at the intruder. Mrs Honour's grey dress and silver eyes shimmered in the firelight. The nurse experienced a tightness of apprehension in her chest. Her mind raced as she tried to understand what the older woman meant.

'I'm sorry?' she stammered.

Mrs Honour snapped back, 'And so you should be.' She stared into Nurse Smythson's eyes with a frighteningly manic gaze. 'My son will marry Lady Clarke.'

Nurse Smythson realised that nothing good could come of this encounter and determined to leave as soon as possible, 'Excuse me,' she stated calmly and stepped towards the door, hoping to sweep past Mrs Honour and make a dignified exit.

She had only just moved beyond the older woman when she felt a cord slip round her neck.

Instinctively she raised her hands, clawing at the cord as it tightened, squeezing the breath out of her. Her fingers moved wildly and futilely as her airways closed. Fear and lack of oxygen sent her heart racing. Dizziness and weakness threatened to engulf her.

*I must be able to fight her off,* thought Nurse Smythson frantically, but the more she struggled the tighter the cord was pulled, mercilessly cutting into her neck's soft white flesh. Her stomach tightened and panic overtook her as she realised, *I am going to die.*

Just as all was going black, she heard Dr Honour's voice. 'Susan, darling, thinking about it, I'm sure it would be fine if—' He broke off abruptly, then yelled, 'Mother!' His voice sounded like a thunderclap, vibrating around the room and filling Nurse Smythson's spirits with hope.

Through a dizzy haze, she heard Mrs Honour being struck and felt the cord loosen. Relief was still in the future; for now she sank to the ground, gasping for life.

Footsteps echoed; she was aware of voices. *Is that Busby? Mrs Farrington?* But what she was most conscious of was Victor's arms holding her, cradling her and lovingly protecting her.

Slowly, for Nurse Smythson, the room began to come into focus. There seemed to be half the village crammed into the small room, making it even harder for her to breathe.

The doctor realised she was struggling to fill her lungs when all around people were gawking and murmuring. She was extremely grateful for the way he firmly ushered everyone but a few out.

Above the hubbub she could make out Mrs Honour's hysterical explanations. 'No! No! Let go of me! You don't understand – she has to die. My son has to marry Lady Clarke!'

Flora stared at Mrs Honour. Her dress and hair were still immaculate, but her eyes were wild and spittle dripped from her mouth as she struggled against Busby's restraining arms.

'You are all fools!' spat Mrs Honour with a gleam of triumph in her manic gaze. 'None of you guessed that my papa was involved with Nurse Smythson's father's supplying those infamous army boots. None of you enquired into my maiden name.'

Nurse Smythson frowned. 'Does that mean that he was also in business with Maud Adams' father?'

Mrs Honour let out a high-pitched hysterical laugh. 'Of course he was! That's why Maud was a problem until she died. She found out, you see.'

Busby seemed to have found a way to secure Mrs Honour's arms behind her back. She was deflated, her struggles ebbing to a limp wriggling.

'I need to ring for a police car and extra officers,' declared Busby.

'Already done, sir,' stated Roberts, calmly. 'If I may make a suggestion. While we wait for the car, she can be secured downstairs; part of the wine cellar has an alcove which has iron bars and can be padlocked.'

'Spiffing idea!' enthused Flora. 'The family has always used it to keep the odd precious bottle of Napoleon brandy so Mrs Honour will be as safe as houses. What's more, it comes complete with a comfortable armchair and it has the added bonus that it is far away from the villagers' eyes.'

Roberts took over Busby's grip on Mrs Honour, leaving the inspector free to readjust his smart black-tie ensemble.

Dr Honour inclined his head, his eyes sad but accepting, resigned to the situation he murmured, 'I'll stay with her.'

Nurse Smythson placed a hand on Dr Honour's arm and added, 'I will too.'

Flora nodded. 'Jolly good idea; that will really annoy her.'

Busby gave her a look.

'Oops! Did I say that out loud?' grimaced Flora.

'Yes,' said Busby, trying not to smile.

Mademoiselle Jacqueline, who had up until now had been watching from the sidelines decided that now was the time for her starring moment. She glided up to Busby. 'Oh Claudius, you are *so* brave,' she declared, her voice a little breathy. Delicately, she swooned into his arm. He caught her adeptly and stared down at her. Her large blue eyes gazed up at him, her impossibly long dark lashes fluttering becomingly.

Defeated by youth and general Frenchness, Flora slunk back. She glanced over at the mistletoe and muttered, 'Fat lot of good you've been – and after all the trouble I had collecting you, too.'

Busby ordered everyone out of the library. Flora had no doubt he would be busy for the rest of the evening, locking Mrs Honour up, dealing with the back-up police officers and generally being rather marvellous.

Debo paused to exclaim with rapture, 'Isn't it wonderful, Mummy? Everything is sorted and Paul Draycott will be home for Christmas.'

'Yes, it's wonderful, darling,' agreed Flora without much enthusiasm. Her daughter was too excited to notice her apathy; she turned on her heels and ran out of the room.

Flora sat alone and miserable. She sighed then looked up and was surprised to see Busby in the doorway. 'So you've managed to tear yourself way from Mademoiselle oh-so-pert-and-French Jacquline?'

The fine lines around his hazel eyes crinkled as he smiled. 'I don't need to be much of a detective to realise you are jealous.'

Outraged, Flora rouse to her full height, threw her head back and jutted her chin out defiantly. 'Me? Don't be ridiculous!'

If anything, his smile deepened. He took a step towards her, his hand going into his pocket. 'So, if I am being ridiculous, am I still allowed to give you your Christmas present?'

For a second Flora's thoughts were fuzzy and unfocused. She experienced a small fluttering in her tummy and her heart beat a little faster. Happiness started to well up deep inside her. 'A present? For me?' She took a couple of steps towards him. 'Oh, you shouldn't have – where is it?'

Laughing he took out a small box-shaped gift, beautifully wrapped in paper with a red ribbon. It was obviously a jewellery box. Flora's eyes widened and her mouth went dry. 'It's not a...' she swallowed and took a breath before finishing with '...a ring?'

Now it was his eyes that widened. Startled horror was all too evident on both his face and in his voice. 'No – it's a brooch.'

'Much more sensible,' she said hurriedly.

Taking it in her trembling hands she hastily unwrapped it. It was a beautiful gold dachshund with a bright ruby eye. Now her heart was racing, and happy adrenaline flooded her body making her skin flush and her eyes sparkle. Beaming, she looked into his eyes, 'Gosh, how lovely.'

Feeling suddenly shy, she reached for a small package she had hidden away under a cushion of her favourite armchair. She handed it to him, murmuring, 'Your gift isn't a surprise, but here.'

He smiled and unwrapped the shiny stainless-steel hip flask.

'Thank you,' was all he said but Flora felt a whole flotilla of butterflies flutter in her stomach.

*Gosh! Who'd have thought that exchanging gifts like this – just the two of us in front of the fire with the distant sound of the band playing – would feel so...* She hesitated while she summoned the right word. *So intimate?*

With unaccustomed coquettishness, she glanced at him from under her eyelashes, then her eyes went to the mistletoe. Her voice was low and husky as she whispered, 'Let me thank you properly.'

Simultaneously they moved close to each other. She could

hear his breath was harder than normal. Gently he brushed a curl away from her cheek. His touch was light and warm. She leaned into him, tilting her head up, her eyes closed. She totally abandoned herself to the moment. There was no one but Busby in her world until:

'*Mummy*!' Debo's voice was high-pitched and excited.

Busby and Flora sprang apart. Flora was too startled by this sudden interruption to be able to draw her scattered thoughts of loss and disappointment together.

'Oh Mummy, there you are. And hello, Busby, fancy you being here too.' She paused for a moment and tilted her head on one side as she regarded her slightly dishevelled mother. 'I say, are you alright? You are positively scarlet.'

'Er—' was all Flora managed to say before Debo carried on.

She spoke rapidly, waving a piece of paper above her head. 'You'll never guess what has happened. I went to Lavinia's room because I was cold and she had said I could borrow her stole if I got chilly, and would you believe it, it wasn't there!'

By now Flora had had enough time to register exactly what her daughter had interrupted between herself and Busby, and there was a note of exasperation in her voice as she snapped, 'Lavinia is probably wearing it herself.'

'Oh, Mummy, do let me finish! Not only was her stole not there but all her other clothes and bits and bobs were gone. The only thing left was this letter to you.' She waved the paper more vigorously.

Flora was just wondering, why, if the letter was addressed to her, Debo had taken it upon herself to read it, when her daughter made an announcement that left her reeling.

'She's run off – I suppose you would say eloped. Generally, all very romantic but she's only gone and picked Mr Adams to be her *grand amour*.' She screwed up her face in disgust. 'Mr Adams – yuck! The letter gushes about him being the love of her life and lots of soppy stuff like that.' She held her head on one side as she quizzed Flora and Busby. 'Have *you* ever noticed the sad nobility in Mrs Adams' eyes? I can't say that I have.'

It was at this moment that Gigi swept in, a concerned look on her face and the beautiful boys by her side. She frowned. 'I am afraid it's all rather more serious than that. Derek Adams must have realised we were on to him.'

Busby sprang to attention. 'Realised you were on to him?'

Gigi gave him a curt look. 'Yes, the boys and I have been keeping a close eye on him ever since I became suspicious of the legacies that Mrs Pie received at regular intervals. When we looked into it, they were all from women who died leaving a heartbroken husband. Our focus soon fell on Maud's Derek. Derek Adams is just the name he is calling himself at the moment. He's been using a variety of names and personas over the years. I believe he is a serial marrier and the murderer of young heiresses.'

'But why?' stammered Flora, 'It's not like he got a penny in Maud's will.'

'Nor did he in any of his other wives' wills.'

'Then why? What on earth was his motivation?'

Gigi expression was almost gleeful. 'Freud or Jung would have a field day with a study of him. He was one of Mrs Pie's boys – it was through her I first became suspicious of him. All of his wives are like his own mother: pretty and frivolous. She took her own life after yet another failed great love affair. Mrs Pie says he never got over it. Somewhere in his twisted mind he felt he was being kind to his victims.'

'That sounds a bit loopy,' announced Debo.

'While they were alive, he lavished all the love and attention on them that his mother always craved.'

'But then he murdered them?' Flora stated in disbelief.

Gigi nodded. 'The ultimate revenge on the mother who abandoned him.'

Debo had been listening to Gigi with open-mouthed fascination. 'Gosh, he has quite a saviour complex – rescuing his wives from their longing for affection, bumping them off and then nobly giving the money to Mrs Pie.'

Flora gasped. 'Oh my! Lavinia!'

Busby looked at Flora and enquired, with more than a hint

of irritation, 'What is it with your family and their reluctance to involve the police?' He glared at Gigi with angry eyes, his voice was hard, 'You do realise that if you had done the right thing and come to me with this information we could have investigated it and Lavinia would not be in danger.'

Gigi glowered at Busby. 'Inspector, that's a little harsh. I was going to talk to you the moment I had proof rather than mere suspicions. But this is not the time for recriminations. You and Flora had better go after Derek Adams and Lavinia. The boys and I will man the phone and call for reinforcements.'

Debo stepped forward. She held her chin high, her shoulders were back and there was a gleam in her eye as she grinned at her mother. 'Before you dash off and rescue Lavinia, Mummy, can we just acknowledge I was right? I did find the vital clue.' She was honest enough to add with a shrug, 'Only I didn't know it was a clue.'

'I'm sure you were totally right, dear, but can we discuss it later? I am just a tad busy right now.' Flora then had a flashback of when she had brushed Debo off in a similar way before she went missing. She paused, 'What I meant to say, darling, was, "Yes dear?"'

'I saw a photo in the Adams' bedroom of the beautiful lady and the little boy and then I saw the same little boy at Mrs Pie's home.'

Flora laughed and placed an affectionate kiss on the top of her daughter's head. 'You are, indeed, a remarkable young sleuth.'

'Hate to interrupt,' said Busby dryly, 'but could we make a move?'

'Quite, quite,' agreed Flora. She made for the door then stopped. 'But we don't know where they are going, so how do we know what direction to go?'

Debo jumped up and down with glee as she waved the letter some more. 'It's all in here! They are taking the Victory from Southampton to South Africa and plan to be married at sea by the captain. Apparently, that's romantic.'

'Right so it's off to Southampton we go!' said Flora

'One more thing Mummy.' Called Debo as her mother made for the door.

'Yes dear.' Called Flora over her shoulder.

'When you do catch up with Mr Adams, could you give him a good kick on the shins from me?'

Confused Flora stopped and turned to face her daughter, 'Why?'

'Well, it must have been him who tried to drown me, the rotter.'

'Will do darling.' Asserted Flora as she swept out the door.

'And I'll alert the police to all of this,' said Gigi calmly, 'And could someone get me another glass of champagne?'

# CHAPTER 18

*THE CHASE*

As Flora and Busby dashed to grab their hats and coats, Busby said, 'You'd better drive.'

Surprised, Flora glanced at him.

He shrugged. 'You are far faster than me.' As she started to beam, he added, 'And more reckless.'

'I'll take that as a compliment,' she said, pulling on her hat and gloves.

They lost no time in opening the garage doors and starting the engine. Just before they plunged into the night, Flora felt Busby's hand on her arm. She looked over at him. In the half-light, she had to blink to see him clearly. His eyebrows were drawn together. His hazel eyes were serious. He looked deeply into her eyes, in a way that made Flora's heart skip and her tummy tighten.

When he spoke, his voice was low and serious. 'Promise me that when we catch up with Derek Adams and Lavinia, you won't put yourself at risk by trying to be a hero.'

Flora's reply was lost in the roar of the engine, as she put her foot flat on the accelerator and they tore down the drive.

Moments later they were speeding down the country lanes, the icy air stung Flora's cheeks but she hardly noticed; it was taking all her concentration to keep the Morgan on the slippery road. Either side of the twisting lanes she glimpsed stone walls and the tall outline of bare beech trees. Their waving branches reminded Flora of sinister skeleton fingers illuminated by the silver light of the moon. The engine slowed slightly when confronted with going up the many steep hills but fairly flew when they were going down.

Using all her skill to drive as fast as she could without having an accident, her mind briefly strayed. *How could I not have noticed the whirlwind romance going on under my nose? Poor, foolish Lavinia, we simply have to rescue her.*

But with each extra mile that passed without sight of Derek Adams' car, Flora's adrenaline began to ebb. Her hope, if not her determination, began to falter.

'One good thing about a Christmas Eve car chase is that we have the roads to ourselves. Everyone is tucked up at home with something warming to drink.' She spoke with a lot more brightness than she felt but she didn't have bothered to put on a false front of optimism as her words were carried away by the wind.

Busby shouted back, 'What?'

Flora couldn't be bothered to reply.

Eventually, just as Flora was giving up all hope, they saw a car ahead. It was driving at speed and erratically. As it swerved this way and that, only just managing to stay on the road, she thought, *Typical man, driving above their skill level.* Just to confirm what she was already certain of, she shouted over to Busby, 'Do you think that's them?'

Above the noise of the engine, he replied, 'I can't imagine anyone else would be driving at such breakneck speed on this road on Christmas Eve.'

They followed the other car, gaining on them all the time.

'Now if we can just follow them—' Busby began, but Flora was already taking advantage of a wider stretch of road and attempting to draw alongside them. She heard him take a gasp of air and thought he yelled her name.

For her part she was assessing the road ahead, what little of it she could make out. In her mind she charted the route she wanted the Morgan to take. She felt a surge of confidence in her own ability to manoeuvre her vehicle and a steely determination to save Lavinia from Derek Adams.

They were alongside each other now. Flora glanced over and saw Derek. He was gripping the steering wheel as if his life depended on it and his face was contorted with unmistakable rage. Lavinia was in the seat beside him, waving frantically at Flora. Her mouth was open and although Flora couldn't hear it, she knew that she was screaming.

*That should give Derek Adams a headache,* Flora thought with satisfaction.

Derek swerved, then corrected himself.

Flora clenched her jaw and stared ahead. She was dimly aware of Busby gripping the sides of the Morgan, his foot pressed down, presumably in an instinctive attempt to find a brake.

Flora had already decided to run Derek's car off the road and she no intention of allowing anyone or anything get in the way. She edged her car forward until the bonnet was a nose in front of the other car. With great deliberation, she swung her car towards Derek's vehicle. They were so close that Busby could see the whites of Lavinia's terrified eyes and, had he wished, he could have touched the other car.

Derek's nerve cracked before Flora's did. His car veered off the road and into a nearby ditch.

Flora gave a whoop of delight and Busby thanked the good Lord that he was still alive. Slamming on the brakes, she brought her car to a screeching stop.

Busby leapt out and turned to run towards the other car. It was wedged half in and half out of the ditch, but despite this Derek Adams had already scrambled out of it.

Even by the dim light of the moon, Flora could make out that his face was puce and drenched in perspiration. He must have been breathing heavily as she could see his shoulders were heaving up and down. Most alarming of all was the gun he was holding. He was levelling it at Busby.

Dread flooded Flora. For a microsecond, her eyes widened and she felt dizzy. Simultaneously, she heard a gunshot and her own scream echo across the night-cloaked countryside.

Busby gasped. His hands went to his chest, then his knees buckled and he crumpled to the ground by her feet.

Horror flooded every atom of Flora. She could hear the rush

of her own pulse in her ears, she couldn't catch her breath and seemed totally frozen with horror, unable even to blink.

She wanted to shout, 'No! No! No!' but no words would come out.

Even in the dim light she could see an evil smile of satisfaction playing around Derek Adams' thin lips. As she watched, Lavinia loomed behind him. With a mighty swing of her overnight case, she hit him over his head with enough force to stun him. The gun dropped from his hand.

With a speed that made Flora proud to be her godmother, Lavinia picked up the gun, and with determination pointed it at Derek.

She had obviously changed her mind about Derek being the love of her life as she snarled, 'Feel free to move, as nothing would give me greater pleasure than to have an excuse to shoot you.'

With Derek secured, Flora fell to her knees beside Busby's inert body. As tears streamed down her face, she gently lifted his head on to her knee.

She ran her hands through his russet curls, all the time murmuring, 'This can't be happening. Why didn't I tell you how I feel about you?'

She became aware of an approaching car just moments before she was dazzled by headlights.

The moment the car screeched to a stop, Dr Honour and Nurse Smythson leapt out, shortly followed the lumbering and less nimble, Nanny.

Dr Honour assessed the situation with a glance and went to assist Lavinia while Nurse Smythson sped over to Flora and Busby.

Nanny regarded Lavinia with a gun, Derek Adams cowering on the ground and Busby's inert body. She took in Flora's distraught state and curtly commanded, 'Leave the poor man alone! Being shot is bad enough without having to put up with you wailing in his ears.'

Before Flora could summon a suitable retort, she felt a slight movement from Busby. His eyes fluttered open, he blinked, focused on Flora and a slow smile spread across his face.

Elation surged through her. Her heart raced and warmth radiated through her body.

Nurse Smythson's clinical voice cut through this tender moment. 'Don't try to move too soon.'

There was no need to give Busby that instruction as he seemed quite content to stay still with his head nestled on Flora's lap. She looked down at him and her tears of joy mingled with her laughter.

With each beat of his heart, Busby regained his senses. It was only now that Flora realised that, despite the gunshot, there was no blood.

Eventually, with Nurse Smythson's help, Busby sat up. Smiling at Flora, his voice slightly husky, he said, 'It's alright, I'm fine – just slightly winded.'

'But how?' she stammered. 'I saw Derek Adams shoot you.'

He chuckled and stiffly reached for his breast pocket. Slowly, he took out the steel hip flask which was now severely dented. 'It seems that your Christmas present saved my life.'

Flora grinned. 'So glad it came in handy.'

# CHAPTER 19

## *TYING UP LOOSE ENDS*

There were many things Flora had to adjust to in the weeks following Christmas. Probably the most challenging was the way Mrs Scrubs seemed to have taken up residence at Farrington Hall. *I must remember to call her Coco or – to use her full stage name – Coco, the Cat Lady.* While Flora found it admirable that Aunt Gigi, Anton and Pierre had taken it upon themselves to launch Mrs Scrubs' stage career, she could not help wishing they would do it elsewhere. It was unnerving, to say the least, to walk into one's drawing room to find Mrs Scrubs and the beautiful boys rehearsing. Often, she would be singing a tuneful duet or as now, practising the Charleston in the library.

*Although, I must say, the transformation has been nothing short of miraculous. There's no trace of a tortoise about her now, what with her bobbed ginger curls, fashionable, if rather flamboyant clothes and more make up than even Lavinia wore in her most frivolous days.*

*I think it's admirable the way she's using Aunt Gigi's contacts in prestigious periodicals to raise awareness of the shame and plight suffered by innocent illegitimate children. When she told us of her childhood, even Nanny had a tear in her eye and quite excused her fibbing.*

Dorothy, with her dog ability to read her mistress's thoughts gave a low growl. *That being said,* thought Flora, *I wish, if she must spend time here, she would leave her cat at home.*

Gigi turned to Lavinia. 'So, now the dust has settled, have you given any more thoughts as to what you are going to do with your life?'

Looking a beguiling combination of breathtakingly pretty and earnest, Lavinia nodded. 'Oh rather.'

The room fell silent; all eyes were on her. The gramophone had come to its end as had Anton's dance lesson with Mrs Scrubs.

'I feel my previous life lacked gravitas,' she began solemnly.

'Gravitas?' queried Gigi.

Lavinia nodded. 'Gravitas means seriousness, dignity, solemnity of manner.'

'Oh, I know what it means; I am just surprised you do.' Gigi smiled encouragingly at Lavinia. 'Go on child, I didn't mean to interrupt.'

'Well, when Derek Adams was an injured, tragic widower, rather than a scheming, manipulative wife-killer, I rather enjoyed fussing around him and being useful.' Here she paused and looked around at the assembled company with her large blue eyes. 'Why did no one ever tell me how enjoyable it is to be useful?' She batted her long dark eyelashes, which added emphasis to her query.

Gigi grunted. 'I imagine being useful was a novel experience for you.'

'Totally.' Lavinia nodded. 'And then after I saw Nurse Smythson being simply splendid, always so sure of herself, so composed, I decided I am going to be a nurse.'

Surprised Flora stammered, 'Are you sure it's what you want, dear? I mean there's bound to be a lot of scrubbing and whatnot.'

Lavinia nodded some more. 'Oh yes, I'm quite decided. The only thing I have my doubts about is the uniform. And obviously I refuse to wear ugly, sensible shoes.'

'Quite,' said Gigi. 'And talking of sensible shoes, any news of Mrs Honour?'

Flora sighed. 'That poor lady has quite lost her marbles; it looks like she will need a long stay in a caring institution. I say Aunt Gigi, while I think of it, when you came across Mrs Honour here you said you'd met her before—'

Gigi shrugged. 'I was mistaken, I hadn't actually met her before, but I think she has one of evil souls that always reminds one of other wicked people one has met before, hence my mistake. If you ask me, an institution is the best place for her. It'll be such a blessing for

Dr Honour and Nurse Smythson to have her out of the way.' She grinned. 'I do have some good news for them. I had a word with some of my chums and we will be able to fund Dr Honour's Home for Heroes.'

'That *is* good news,' said Flora, without mentioning that she was one of the generous donors. 'And what about Mrs Pie?'

A flicker of sadness crossed Gigi's face. 'The poor dear is devastated by the behaviour of one of her boys. She has been visiting him in prison every week without fail, but she is philosophical by nature and will get over it.'

'Does she feel badly about having profited from murder?' enquired Lavinia.

Gigi gave out a guffaw of laughter. 'Hardly. She is far too practical for that.'

Mrs Scrubs went to flop down on the sofa and then corrected herself so that she sat with grace.

*Gigi has obviously been giving her lessons in deportment as well as dancing and singing,* thought Flora as she shuffled a little along the sofa to allow more space for both them both. *I must say, she has made the transition from skivvy to equal with surprising ease.* Mrs Scrubs sniffed, suggesting that her education in manners was still a work in progress.

'From everything I've heard, it would have been more fun for me had I been raised by Mrs Pie in her home rather than my spiteful aunts, who kept on at me about my shameful birth.'

'No doubt,' said Anton, passing her a cup of tea.

'You have a duty to make up for your unhappy start by making sure your golden years are glorious. No regrets,' added Pierre, handing her a generous slice of cake.

Anton sighed. 'Some regrets are unavoidable. As Gigi said, we were looking into Derek Adams. If only we'd arrived a little earlier the day Maud Adams was murdered.'

Flora, thinking to herself *Ah, so that explains the story about the angels in the village on that day,* gave him a sympathetic look. 'I think Derek Adams was so set on murder that there was nothing you could have done. It is possible that the amount of morphine he had stolen from Nurse Smythson's bag would have been enough to kill Maud even without the lake. In that case you could never have kept watch every moment they were together.'

Pierre nodded and added, 'It was difficult keeping an eye on him, especially before we were staying here.'

'I was wondering about that.' Confessed Flora. 'Where were you before you came here? There aren't any guesthouses locally.'

'We made our base in Oxford, it's a big enough town that we could be fairly anonymous but there was a lot of travelling.'

Mrs Scrubs looked thoughtful 'At the fireworks- who shot Derek Adams?'.

'Noone,' smiled Anton. 'Mr Adams needed to make himself look like a victim and put further blame on Paul.'

Pierre took up the story, 'So he cut his own ear, let off a shot and dropped the gun by Paul who unfortunately picked it up when he saw it.'

Mrs Scrubs shook her head sadly, 'He really wasn't as charming as I thought,' she paused before adding, 'Something else that I have been pondering, if Mr Adams always had his wives leave their money to Mrs Pie's children's home, how did he live? He was always going away on business, but I never saw any actual evidence of him working.'

Gigi took a sip of tea. 'He always made sure the marital home was in his name, then as a distraught widower he would sell it, saying it had too many memories.'

'Talking of memories,' said Flora, 'Christmas is in the past and I really must get rid of that.'

She nodded towards the bunch of mistletoe which was still hanging up.

'I'll help get it down,' offered Pierre as he put a chair under the festive posy and nimbly climbed on to it. A minute later he handed Flora the bunch of foliage with its pearly white berries.

She took it with a sigh. 'What a waste,' she muttered as she carried it out of the room with Dorothy on her heels.

They were passing through the hall when there came a familiar knock on the front door. Flora's heart instantly began to beat faster, and Dorothy's tail started to wag,

She opened the door and there he was. When he saw them both, Busby's smile lit up his whole face. Dorothy's happiness exploded: she wiggled, barked and jumped up at his trouser legs. He broke his gaze away from Flora's eyes to Dorothy's, 'Alright old girl.' He laughed, picking her up and letting her nuzzle under his chin while he cooed to her, 'Yes, you are the most beautiful dachshund in the world and yes, I do love you very much.'

Flora felt a pang of jealousy towards Dorothy.

He put the dog down and ignoring her little yaps of protest, he stepped inside, shuttled the door behind him.

Taking his hat and gloves off, he looked at Flora with a gleam in his fox-brown eyes, 'Mrs Farrington – Flora – I think we have some unfinished business.'

'We do?' she queried, fluttering her eyelashes in a way that would have made Mademoiselle Jacqueline blush. She took a step closer to him, so near that she caught a pleasant whiff of his cologne. She fancied she could hear his heart beating, but it might have been her own. 'Whatever can that be? Paul Draycott has been exonerated.'

Busby put an arm around her waist and gently pulled her towards him. His body was warm and firm against hers. It was a good thing he was holding her tightly as she feared her knees were giving way. She swallowed.

His voice was husky as he replied, 'Yes, and I gather he is now working for you.'

Flora nodded. 'And I can't wait to see,' her voice caught as he gently stroked her face while all the time gazing intensely into her eyes, 'what he does with my roses.'

'I'm sure they will be magnificent,' he murmured, 'but that wasn't the business I was referring to.'

'It wasn't?' asked Flora innocently as she encircled her arms around his neck. She let the mistletoe drop; somehow, she didn't feel it was needed.

He tilted his head as she reached up. Their lips touched…

Printed in Dunstable, United Kingdom